LIBERATING WATER

International Bestselling Author

ELIZABETH KNIGHT

Knight, Elizabeth
Liberating Water

Editing: Swish Editing & Design
Cover artist: RYN KATRYN BOOK COVERS
Formatting: Creative Wonder Publishing

CHAPTER I

LAILAH

"We finished the serum today. It was ready to be tested, and we made a batch of twenty vials. They're gone," Chadwick said, his British accent becoming stronger in his distress.

I sat stunned on the hotel couch between Hudson and Brayden. This was worse than we thought. Not only had we discovered that the Dark Lord has a hidden army, but he now had the one tool he needed to make more soldiers for it. Watching Hudson's father start to fray at the edges of his perfectly maintained exterior made my heart ache for him. I wanted to reach out and comfort him, but seeing as we only met a few hours ago, I didn't think he would welcome it.

Pulling himself upright, he gathered his thoughts and stood. "If you will excuse me, it seems that I must be getting back to the facility. There is an investigation that needs to be done. We must find out who took the Day-Brite formula." Chadwick turned to Brayden's father, Oliver, gripping his shoulder. "Please tell Adriana I'm sorry."

With that he left the room in a hurry, phone to his ear, talking to someone in what sounded like French. I turned to

Hudson and found his face void of emotion, but his mouth was tight, as if he was holding himself back from following. His honey blond hair that was typically styled to perfection was mussed, and his bright blue eyes were guarded. Pushing his glasses back up his nose, I saw his hand shake with the need to do something.

"Hudson, you need to be with him," I said softly, taking his hand. "We will stay here tonight, so go take care of your father."

Hudson held my face in his hands and placed a kiss on my forehead. "I'll be back in the morning."

I nodded, waving for him to follow after his father. "Go."

Hearing the door close after Hudson, I sagged against Brayden, the events of the evening catching up to me. Battling a demon-enhanced warrior from the Dark Lord's army sure takes a lot out of a girl. Never had I expended that much power, or been attacked quite so viciously. It had taken me shampooing my hair three times to get all the blood out of it. Made me jealous of Jay's shaved head.

"Father, I think it's best if we turn in for the evening. We can talk more tomorrow when we're rested. There isn't much we can do at this point," Brayden said, wrapping an arm around me.

It was moments like this that the connection we had by being bonded was very useful. I knew he could feel how exhausted I was through my emotions. Not that he was much better—the worry he had about his mother was chipping away at any energy reserves he had. When I glanced at my other three boys, they all looked ragged too.

Even Jay was sitting on the edge of the couch. For some this wouldn't be a big deal, but Jay always preferred to stand. His dark gray eyes, that typically were alert and watchful, drooped slightly, making their almond shape more pronounced. Micah sat next to him, head tossed back, staring at the ceiling with his signature scowl. His thick brown hair was loose around his shoulders when he typically kept it up. Then there was Parker, the man who looked at life as a big party or game to play. His bright orange-red hair was still damp from his shower and flat on his head instead of styled in his signature spiked faux-hawk look. As if he knew I was watching him, he looked up at me from where he was sitting on the floor, leaning against my legs. His brown eyes were missing that teasing glint as he gave me a half-hearted grin.

I didn't like how defeated everyone looked right now. I clearly needed to do something about it.

"Of course, you're right. We can meet over breakfast and figure out the next course of action," Oliver said, slapping his hands on his knees and standing. "Come along Makoto, Tobias. Let the kids get some sleep. They worked hard tonight keeping us safe."

Jay's dad, Makoto, slowly stood and opened his mouth like he was going to say something to his son but thought better of it. Nodding to us all, he shuffled off in his yukata and slippered feet.

Tobias walked past Parker and ruffled his hair, giving him the grin Parker had inherited. "G'night son, proud of you."

Once the dads left and it was just us in the room, emotions were heavy in the air, thick with defeat. Pulling myself away from Brayden, I stood and walked to the other side of the coffee table, taking them in.

"Why do you guys look like a bunch of kicked puppies?" I asked, placing my hands on my hips. "Did I just come from a different battle where we didn't kick that creepy woman's ass?"

Micah, of course, was the first to glare at me with his sapphire eyes. "Did you not just hear what happened? What we did doesn't matter."

"Bullshit it doesn't matter, Micah!" I snapped. "We saved Brayden's mother from possibly being turned into one of those things. Besides, if we hadn't gotten that information from

Tabitha, how long would it have taken Chadwick to check his office?"

"She makes a valid point," Jay said, standing up and starting to pace behind the couch. "There is a very small window in which the Day-Brite serum could have been taken."

"Thank you, Jay, for seeing my side of this," I said, giving him a soft smile. "Can we also talk about what happened during that fight?"

"You mean the armor thing?" Parker asked with a hint of his real grin. "That was pretty sweet! What do you think brought that on?"

The three boys all looked at Parker like he was an idiot, and Micah slapped him upside the head. "Lailah, you moron."

"Fuck off, a lot happened all at once," Parker said, getting up and shoving Micah over, then taking a seat on the couch. "Notice she isn't bringing up the fact that she almost bled to death right before that."

Now I was the one that was under their scrutiny. I raised my hands in surrender, trying to hold back my grin of triumph that I'd pulled them out of their pity party.

"Who would have guessed that she could gather that much demonic energy? Let alone try and pull the small bit I have out of me," I said, defensively.

"Is that what she was doing?" Micah asked, leaning forward, his eyes swirling with anger.

I shrugged my shoulders. "It's the only thing I can think of. It felt like she was trying to pull something out of me that definitely didn't want to leave."

"It could have been your heart. You know, like the wicked stepmother from Snow White," Parker suggested.

I could see Micah gearing up to smack Parker again, so I interjected. "Whatever it was, we stopped it and I'm fine. Let's get some sleep before something else happens and we're running on empty."

Parker groaned, flopping against the couch. "Why would you even put that into the universe, Trouble? So not cool."

I chuckled as I headed into one of the bedrooms that had the king-size bed. Tossing off the extra pillows, I pulled back the covers and got settled in the middle of the big bed. A few minutes later, Brayden crawled in next to me and pulled me against him, intertwining our legs. I tucked my head under his chin, and we both let out a heavy sigh.

"You scared the shit out of me, Lailah," Brayden whispered after we had been lying there for a few minutes in silence. "I could feel how much pain you were in, and I couldn't do anything to help you."

I wrapped my arms around his waist, clutching him to me. "You did do something—you saved me. If you all hadn't placed a hand on me, I don't think I would have survived."

He kissed the top of my head, then my forehead, the tip of my nose, and then our lips met. I could feel his need for reassurance that I was truly okay. This wasn't about sex; it was purely the need to hold me. I surrendered to him, giving him what he needed—what we both needed.

"I didn't know how much I was truly in love with you until I thought you were going to leave me," Brayden said, pulling me away so he could look me in the eyes.

I felt my eyes widen at his words. "Brayden, did you just declare your love for me?"

"Apparently not very well if you're questioning it," Brayden said, love and laughter in his gaze. "Lailah Mackenzie, I am hopelessly in love with you."

My chest burst with the happiness and love that flooded my body. I couldn't tell if it was from him or if it was me... not that it mattered, since the feeling was mutual. This time I could say it in return.

"Brayden Dolton, I love you too," I admitted seconds before his lips came crashing onto mine.

We made out until both our lips were swollen and red from being nibbled, bit, and sucked. Neither of us had much energy to do anything else, but with our connection, there was no doubting how we each felt about each other. Finally, we both found ourselves drifting off to sleep, my hands under his shirt planted on the skin of his back, while he wrapped his arms around my waist.

Sometime later, I was awoken when I felt someone climbing into the bed on my other side. I cracked an eye and found Micah, who was pulling up the covers and laying on his back beside me.

"You okay?" I murmured, untangling myself to face him.

"Couldn't sleep," Micah said gruffly.

"Want to tell me about it?" I pushed, knowing there was something more. He never showed his vulnerability.

He turned to look at me, and the fear in his eyes shocked me. I'd seen many emotions from Micah, but fear like this hadn't been one of them. I reached out and took his hand, and that seemed to break whatever control he'd been holding onto. Yanking on my arm, he pulled me away from Brayden and across his chest. His breathing was fast and uneven, like he was on the verge of having a panic attack.

"Shhh, it's okay. We're all safe. We made it out in one piece," I murmured as I combed my fingers through his hair.

"You can't leave me, Lailah," Micah rasped.

I squeezed him tighter as his words almost made me cry. "I'm not going anywhere, Micah. You're not going to get rid of me that easily."

"I won't be able to survive if another person I care about dies. Losing my parents nearly broke me, and I haven't let anyone else in besides Brayden," Micah said, talking quickly. "I don't know how it happened, but you somehow forced your way into my heart, and I can't lose you too."

I pulled Micah's face away from my neck and looked into his eyes before I kissed him. Unlike my kisses with Brayden, Micah's was desperate, clutching at me, fisting my shirt in his hands. I held onto his face, cupping his jaw in both my hands so he could feel me. Kissing Micah was like a thunderstorm; it was wild, electric, and completely unpredictable. Micah kissed down my neck, biting every so often, making me gasp at the jolts it sent through my body. He started to fumble with my shirt, but I stopped him.

"Micah, wait," I panted.

"Why? You want this, I can tell," he asked, frowning.

I shook my head at him with a smirk on my lips. "Yes, I want you, but I don't want the first time we have sex to be because you're upset. Not to mention that your best friend is right next to us."

"Brayden won't care. I'm sure he'd even join in if he woke up," Micah countered.

I sighed, fighting what my body was crying out for now that he had lit the fire within me. "I'm still going to say no tonight, Micah. As much as it kills me to stop, it's not the right time to do this. I want you to be absolutely sure you want to be with me and are ready to take the Oath, because I don't take sex lightly."

Micah flopped onto his back and ran his hands through his hair before looking back at me. "You're right. It's not fair of me to ask you to give me your heart when I can't offer mine in return."

Leaning forward, I pressed a kiss to his lips. "Thank you."

"Can I still sleep here tonight?" he asked.

"If you think you can manage it, you're more than welcome," I said, letting him snuggle up against me.

Once we got settled, Brayden pressed up against me from behind, wrapping himself around me and nuzzling the back of my neck. I'd never felt so safe or cared for in my life, and this was just the beginning.

CHAPTER 2

HUDSON

I slept fitfully on the couch in Father's room. It had been too late for him to get a flight tonight, but he was able to get on the first flight out in the morning. Oliver had arranged for a driver to get him so he didn't need to worry about that detail. Oliver also sent up another bottle of brandy that we indulged in as we chatted before heading to bed.

"Do you have any idea who it could be?" I asked.

Father looked at me with a frustrated frown. "It's hard to tell, because all of Isabelle's staff have access to my labs, as well as my own staff. That alone expands the pool exponentially. Not to mention that Isabelle isn't going to let me interrogate her people. She will see it as an attack on her leadership."

The divorce had been finalized between them three years ago, but they had been living apart for two years before that. Assets in the company had been the only thing keeping them from doing things sooner, all the legal legwork of dividing everything up taking years. My mother fighting every move my father made didn't help, either.

"What if you have the Elementi head up the investigation? It would keep it bipartisan," I suggested.

"Hmm, that might be an idea. Once I get back and take inventory of everything we've been working on, it will tell me if this was an isolated occurrence or if something else was taken." Father tossed back the last of his brandy. "You really don't need to stay with me, Hudson. I'm sure you would rather be back with the others, after what happened."

"I'm sure they all just went to bed. Besides, the only one that would be worried about me is Lailah," I said, sipping my drink.

Personally, I didn't see the point in drinking, but since Lailah came into her power, I kept finding myself in scenarios where drinking would help take the edge off. When we came out here to help Lailah, I figured it might be a chance for me to relax a little around her. As the others have pointed out many times, I am not good with emotions, neither showing them nor dealing with them. Lailah felt everything so easily; it was stunning to watch. Lately, though, I'd felt myself becoming less pragmatic about everything and deciding to get more involved with the group.

A few nights ago I even lost my temper at Parker, which never happens. Anger was a pointless emotion that did more harm than good. I had far too many experiences seeing it happen in my own family. My parents still fight any time they are even near each other. Hell, they even fought on the phone.

Being factual and analytical was a much more productive way of handling a situation. This is what I had to offer Lailah in our dynamic. She had Brayden and Parker to keep her smiling, Jay to keep her healthy and safe, and Micah, without even real-izing it, was teaching her to be more confident in herself. Even Cami was adding to Lailah's life in more ways than I could. No, I was there to guide her with my knowledge and level thinking.

"Hudson, that can't be true," my father said, resting a hand on my shoulder. "You may not see it, but the five of you have grown closer since she came along. There was a time that you never would have been able to defeat a demon like that. You fought so much amongst yourselves that there was no need to let anyone else do the work. Lailah is good for you all, and not just because she's Synergy."

"We finally have a leader. She doesn't know it yet, but she is the one who is getting everyone to try," I shared, giving my father a small smile.

He nodded his head. "The best leaders are the ones who help bring out the best in the people around them."

"If that's the case, how did things with Mother go so wrong?" I asked, knowing it was a risk.

"I keep telling you that you don't have to continue calling her Mother. She was only ever your stepmother," my father said, deflecting from my question.

"She is the only mother I have really ever known, seeing that you got married when I was three," I pointed out.

"That's fair, I suppose. Are you still going to see her for Christmas?"

"Something tells me that the others will want to help hunt down who took the serum. If that's the case, it would be easier to stay with Mother at the villa. I also wouldn't want to miss spending some time with Ben and Grace," I answered.

Father sat back and looked at me with an odd expression. "What makes you think they'll want to hunt down the serum?"

I gave my father a knowing grin. "If I know anything about Lailah, it's that you don't mess with her people. Adriana is Brayden's mom, therefore someone she considers 'her people.'"

"Fascinating," Father mused, turning that tidbit of information over. "Well, my boy, I am off to bed. I will make sure to say goodbye in the morning before I leave."

"Goodnight, Father. I'm sure it won't be long before we see each other again," I said, watching him walk into the bedroom.

I poured myself another finger of brandy and spread out on the couch. Isabelle was the only example I really had growing up to base my knowledge of relationships on. Many years I've tried to pick apart what happened to see where the marriage had failed. What had my father seen in her to marry her in the first place? There had to be something other than loneliness that would have drawn him in. Isabelle was from old money in France, and her family had been in the pharmaceutical world for almost as long as our own.

Then my thoughts turned to my birth mother, who I didn't have a chance to meet, having died in childbirth. She had been a brilliant scientific mind that made changes in the medical world that still to this day save lives. I have a picture of her and my father from when they got married, and they both looked so happy. They had lived in England, where they met, but when she died, father couldn't bear to be anywhere that reminded him of her. So he brought us down to France, where he started a new branch of the family business.

Thinking of my mother had my thoughts drifting to Lailah. Could I really learn to love someone as amazing as her? The fact that she would have four other people to rely on actually made me feel better. If I failed her, then the others would be there to comfort her and give her what I couldn't. The science behind having multiple partners was actually quite logical. More members to provide for her, and added caretakers for when the female reproduced. Not that I wanted Lailah to have children any time soon, and thanks to medical improvements with implanted birth control, it wasn't something we had to worry about for the next three years.

Finally, the brandy seemed to hit my system and slow my brain down enough that I could fall asleep. I could understand the appeal of drinking now, for situations like this. It took all your choices away from you and made your body comply with the suppressant quality of the alcohol.

CHAPTER 3

LAILAH

Sleeping with two extremely cuddly men was wonderful, but when you woke up and needed to pee like a racehorse, it had its challenges. Brayden had my legs trapped between his, and Micah was sleeping with his head right on my bladder. The more I tried to move, the tighter they held on. I let out a loud groan of frustration that apparently had been loud enough to hear in the living room, because the bedroom door opened and Parker's grinning face appeared.

"Trouble, you are in a bit of a pickle, aren't you?" Parker teased as he sauntered into the room shirtless, sweatpants low on his hips. I would have appreciated the sight of him more if I didn't have more pressing issues.

"It would be rather lovely if you could help me get out of this mess," I begged, waving a hand at my situation. "I have to pee so bad."

"What do I get out of it?" Parker asked, crossing his arms at the end of the bed.

I growled as Micah shifted and nuzzled into my bladder. "Whatever you want! Please, I'm going to pee my pants!"

Parker gave me a wide, toothy grin. "Alright, Trouble. I'll get you free, but you owe me, and you have to do whatever I ask in return."

"Fine, fine, I agree. Now help me!" I said, nodding my head as sweat started to break out on my forehead.

"Be right back," Parker said, heading back out into the living room. A minute later he came back with the ice bucket in hand.

"No! No, Parker! Don't do that! If you do that, even I can't protect you," I hissed, but it was too late.

Parker upended the bucket full of slushy ice water all over Micah's back, causing him to bolt upright, gasping.

"Holy fucking shit!" Micah bellowed.

Hearing Parker snickering, Micah flew off the bed, blessed sword in hand, and lunged for Parker. Being smarter than I gave him credit for, Parker bolted out the door, closing it behind him to slow Micah down. Unable to hang on any longer, I scrambled out of the cold, wet bed and dashed for the bathroom.

"What the hell is going on?" I heard a gravelly Brayden call from the bed.

I smothered my laughter as I relieved myself, waiting to hear the telltale signs that Micah caught up to Parker. When I still didn't hear anything after walking back into the bedroom and finding it empty, I headed to the living room. I paused, seeing a shivering Parker on the small balcony in only his boxers, pounding on the glass door. Micah stood near it with a smirk on his lips, his arms crossed.

The door to the room opened, and Hudson walked in and also took a moment to assess what he was seeing. "Do I even want to know?"

"Probably not, but I'm just glad they aren't actively trying to kill each other," I said, walking over to Hudson. "How's your dad doing?"

Hudson shrugged. "As well as can be expected. He left before the sun was up with an action plan in place."

"Can we help? I know it's your parents' company, but surely

there's something the Elementi can do to assist," I said, grabbing Hudson's hand and twining our fingers together.

Hudson gave my hand a squeeze, and a soft smile appeared on his lips. "Actually, I said the same thing. My mother and her people have open access to his office and lab, so both staffs will need to be looked into. I believe it would be best to have an outside group handle the situation, especially since we know the demons are a part of it."

"So does that mean we're going to your house for Christmas?" I asked with a grin.

I knew we had an opportunity to stay here and to celebrate with Brayden's family, but I felt like so much had happened, it might be better if we didn't. Besides, who wouldn't want to travel more of the world if you had free transportation and a place to stay?

"Yes, it seems that's the way things are turning out. I will have to call my mother to give her a heads up, but I know we have more than enough room in the villa for us all to fit," Hudson said.

"Where exactly does your mother live?" I asked, realizing I didn't even know.

"Nice, right on the coast of France."

I let out a shriek of happiness that seemed to get everyone's attention, causing Jay to come out of the back bedroom. The rest just gawked.

"Micah, let Parker back in before he freezes to death. We need to get back to the house so we can pack. We're going to FRANCE!" I crowed as I did a happy dance.

I heard the sliding glass door open and was promptly scooped up by a frigid Parker, who rolled me up with him in the comforter on the bed.

"Oh my god, I think I might have literally frozen my balls off. They are so far up inside me I'm surprised I'm not talking like a girl," Parker said, shivering around me.

"We don't have time for this! We need to get going, we have important things to do," I grumbled, squirming around in the blanket.

"Nope, you're going to make good on your promise to do whatever I ask. So you are going to be bundled up in here with me until I'm warm enough to know I'm not a eunuch," Parker pouted, snuggling his head against my neck.

Letting out a heavy sigh, I resigned myself to my situation and relaxed.

"You know, there is something you could do to help me warm up faster," Parker said, sliding his icicle hand under my sweatshirt.

"I am not getting naked and letting you grope me like some frat boy," I said, tweaking his nipple.

"Ah! Damn, Trouble, that wasn't what I meant, but I should have thought of that first," Parker grumbled, twisting so he was wrapped around my body, pinning my arms to my sides. "I was going to say we could make out, but now I don't think I'm going to ask. You owe me after that titty twister."

"Is it still called a titty twister if you're a guy?" I asked, getting totally sidetracked. "Isn't it a purple nurple?"

Parker pulled back just enough so we were nose to nose. "God, you really are the perfect woman, aren't you?"

Not letting me answer, he captured my mouth with his, and I hummed against his full, kissable lips. Parker nipped, catching my bottom lip between his teeth and pulling me closer to him before he released it. I chased after him and wiggled one of my arms out of his hold to wrap around his neck. I let my fingers scrape along the back of his neck, making him shiver with pleasure. He grabbed my ass with both hands and pulled it flush with his pelvis so I could feel the swell of his dick. I couldn't hold back—I moaned into his mouth, feeling how thick he was. Now that I had been introduced to good sex, I craved it.

I knew for sure that Parker was no longer cold, as his skin

heated under my touch. His lips were hot as they ran down along my neck and nipped at my jaw. He slid his hand under my shirt again, letting his wide hand trail along my ribs until it stopped right under my breast. I arched into him to be closer, not that it was even possible with how close we were already. My power hummed in delight at the contact, his power reaching out and swirling, caressing me. His power was emotions, and there were a hell of a lot of them flying around right now.

"Sorry to interrupt, but just checking if you still wanted to go to France. If we want to be there in time for Christmas, you're going to need to come up for air," Brayden called from some-where in the bedroom.

My answer was to shove Parker away from me and fling off the blanket. Rolling away and off the bed, I landed on my feet and ran over to Brayden, who caught me with an *oof* when I flung myself at him.

"Let's go to France!" I cheered as Brayden grinned at me.

"Damn, should I be offended that that's all it took to get her to drop me like a hot potato?" Parker muttered as he followed Brayden out of the bedroom.

"Just wait until she finds out we are taking the helicopter back up to the cabin," Micah said with a smug expression.

Wiggling, Brayden set me back on my feet so I could face Micah. "Run that by me one more time?"

"Oh, you mean the part about us taking the helicopter back? Let's hope you don't have an episode and try to crash this aircraft too. It's less forgiving," Micah tossed over his shoulder as he walked into the back bedroom.

My jaw fell open at his comment. "Not cool, Micah!"

"Come on. My father called and said they're waiting on us to have breakfast with them in their suite. Seems he has gathered all the parents so we can share what's going on," Brayden explained as he took my hand and led me out of the room.

I was seated at the large dining room table in the equally giant suite that Brayden's parents were staying in, a plate of food piled high in front of me. Jay had promptly sent me to sit down as he made up the plate for me, saying something about replacing the calories I used last night. My stomach growled, but I waited until everyone was seated at the table before I started. Jay sat on my left and Hudson was to my right, following my lead and waiting for the parents to be seated.

I was thrilled to see Adriana here with us, her hazel eyes bright and clear just like Brayden's. Her silver-gray hair was tucked behind her ears, and she seemed so much more relaxed than the last few times I'd seen her.

"Lailah dear, the boys tell me that you're off to France. I'm sad that we won't get to spend Christmas with you, but there is always next year. Let's hope that things will settle down by then. I have a feeling there's a lot that I'm going to find out I missed and will need to deal with. Please let me know if there is any way that I can help. I already sent my research to the Elementi HQ, so they have that data," Adriana said as frown lines creased her brow. "I can't believe I allowed myself to be manipulated in such an awful way."

Reaching across the table, I grabbed her hand and gave it a squeeze. "I'm just thankful that we were able to help. We will figure this out, I promise."

"That's a hefty promise to make, girl," Makoto interjected. "You might be careful you don't make a promise you can't keep."

Bristling at his words, I turned my gaze to Jay's father. Today he was wearing a dark burgundy yukata, and I wondered if he only wore traditional Japanese clothing. His salt-and-pepper hair was swept back from his face in a neat and orderly fashion, and his wrinkled face showed that the scowl he was giving me was a normal expression.

"I couldn't agree more—I don't make promises I can't keep," I stated and turned back to my food, ignoring the cranky old man.

Jay's hand found my leg, and he gave my thigh a gentle squeeze, causing me to look up at him. His slate-gray eyes watched me intently as if he was checking to see how upset his father had made me. I gave him a smile, stretching to place a kiss on his cheek.

"I'm fine," I whispered, wanting to set him at ease.

Jay's shoulders relaxed, and he picked up his fork and started eating. Looking around, I saw everyone was seated and digging into their own meals.

"It seems that we all have been keeping things to ourselves, and I feel like if we are going to have any chance figuring things out, we need to come clean," Tobias announced once the meal was underway.

"That better not have been directed at me, Tobias Jones," Makoto snapped.

This was going to get us nowhere.

Taking a deep breath, I pushed my seat back and stood up, drawing everyone's attention. "I appreciate all of you trying to start us off on the right foot for this investigation, but I think it's best if we go into it with no preconceived notions. We know a member of the Dark Army was in the lab and took the serum. That's more than enough to go on, and the more time we waste here, the more information we will lose. It has been a pleasure to meet you all, and I truly wish it had been under different circum-stances."

With that, I started for the door, knowing that the boys would be following after me in a moment. There was too much at stake and not enough time to get ahead of it.

CHAPTER 4
LAILAH

Huddled on the roof of the hotel, I took in the helicopter that we were going to take back to the cabin and then to the airport. The perk of having a secret, well-funded organization at your back was the convenience of travel. I wasn't afraid of heights, but all I could think of was every war movie my dad and brothers watched where the helicopter was always the first thing to go down.

"You look concerned," Hudson commented as he stood next to me. "The pilot is very experienced, and we would never put you in danger."

Turning to him, I wrapped my arms around his middle, soaking in his comfort. "I know. I'm more worried about what it's taking us to."

"Lailah, you don't have to keep putting on this brave face for us," Hudson said, pulling me into a tight hug. "I understand not wanting to look weak in front of our parents, but we are in this together, and none of us are prepared for what is to come. The six of us are a team, and we've already proven that we are far stronger together than we are apart."

I couldn't help but think of Tabitha's face of shock and

horror as she realized that she wasn't going to take us down with her. Never in my wildest dreams did I think I would be standing here on the edge of a war with the Dark Lord, only the five of us able to stop him.

"Alright, everyone in!" the pilot called, waving an arm at us.

Tucking low like he instructed us to earlier, we piled into the helicopter, and Jay slid the door shut. He waited for everyone to get buckled in and came over to double check mine before he settled himself. Jay grabbed the headset that was on the hook by his shoulder and motioned for us to do the same.

"Brayden, is the plane ready?" Jay asked.

"Yup. They'll be waiting for us once we get there. Hudson, have you talked to your mom yet?" Brayden questioned.

Hudson nodded. "She is sending a driver to meet us at the airport with a company car. My siblings will be home and can get us settled."

"Shouldn't we be going right to the lab?" I interjected.

"I figured it would be best to drop our stuff off before we head over. The driver will be available to us whenever we need," Hudson said.

We fell into a comfortable silence as I peered out the window, taking in the snow-covered mountains. I was a little sad that I didn't get to see very much of it, but I knew that I could come back any time. Once we landed and hurried into the house to begin packing, I was assured by them all that we didn't need to worry about anything else, that cleaners would come in and set the house to rights once again. There was a procedure with safe houses, and we just needed to lock up as we left.

Finally on the plane, we were able to relax for a little while, seeing as it was an almost six-hour flight. Micah promptly passed out on the couch and Jay pulled out a book and started reading while Parker, Hudson, and Brayden kept me company playing card games. After a few rounds of rummy, I started to get sleepy.

"Come on, Trouble. Let's get you laying down before you pass out on the table here," Parker said, scooping me up before I could argue.

I gave the other two a wave as I was carried off to the back of the plane. Expecting Parker to just drop me off and then head back out, I was surprised when he curled up against me. His large, warm body wrapped around mine was solid and grounding for me. Falling asleep on the plane was making me nervous, seeing as the last time this happened I almost crashed the plane.

"You're safe with me here, Trouble. I'll know if anything happens to you and I'll wake you up," he said, nuzzling the top of my head.

Shifting slightly, I looked up at him. "What do you mean?"

"My element isn't the same as the others'. It's not one that you can see or touch; it's all about feelings. I can give or take away certain emotions from people, but the other part of that is I can control that emotion. Let's take fear, for example—I can take away your fear or I can make you become afraid. Then I could take the fear and turn it up and force someone else to become terrified." Parker paused, taking a shaky breath. "I can do it with any emotion, so if I feel you falling into whatever the Dark Lord uses to mess with you, I'll know. He seems to play on your fears and insecurities, turning them into a reality for your dreams."

His fear of my reaction was written all over his face and the fact he couldn't look me in the eye. If I was anyone else and didn't know him the way I do, it might have worried me that he could play with my emotions, but I wasn't.

Reaching up, I grabbed him by the back of the neck and pulled him down to me so I could kiss him. "Thank you for watching over me."

Parker grinned at me. "Trouble like you should never be left alone."

Snuggling against him, I drifted off to sleep with him running his fingers up and down my arm soothingly.

———

"Little Synergy, did you really think you could hide from me?" The Dark Lord's voice swirled around me in the darkness. "Oh, your Knight is trying very hard to remove my hold on you, but he isn't strong enough yet. So it seems I have you at my mercy for the time being. Isn't that fun?"

Panic started to rise as I felt the Dark Lord's clawed hand run down my back. I'd been trapped in this void before, and the guys always seemed to be able to pull me out with their powers. I tried to call on my golden energy, but the spot where it sat in my chest was empty and cold.

"Do you think they can save you in time? My darkness in you is spreading, and your fight with Tabitha only increased the hold it has on you. It nearly killed you when she tried to call it out of your soul, but it wouldn't give up on such a prey as yourself. Your Knights are but foolish boys trying to protect you from me. If they truly wanted that, then your Fire Knight would have taken the Oath and Bonded with you. Selfish, that was, on his part—how can you trust a man who wouldn't put your best interests above his own? Ah, but be wary of your Spirit Knight. Things of the heart can be so... fickle."

"Shut the hell up," I growled, my anger pushing away all my previous fear. "I trust them with my life. I would do anything for them, and I trust they would do the same for me."

"Is that so? What if I told you that I would spare them if you gave yourself to me?" the Dark Lord taunted. "Once I have the world under my rule, you would be free to rejoin them and live happily together."

Scoffing at his words, I shook my head. "Why would I ever believe a word that you tell me? Get the fuck away from me."

"Very well. I will leave you for now, but know that what is to come rests on your shoulders. You could have stopped this all from happening, Little Synergy."

"What do you mean it's not working? You said you could handle it if something went wrong!" Micah's angry voice bellowed.

"I thought I could, but this demonic hold on her is stronger than anything we have ever seen before, so unless you have something to offer, then back the fuck off," Parker growled back, his hands holding my head.

Groaning, I tried to roll out of Parker's hold, feeling like I was going to be sick to my stomach. "I don't feel so good."

There was movement around me, and I was scooped up and carried to the bathroom. I might not have gotten sick if I'd been left alone, but now that I didn't have a choice, I was glad to have the toilet ready. Hands swept my hair back as another rubbed my back in comfort before placing a cool, wet towel around my neck.

Finished heaving my guts out, I slid against the wall of the bathroom, taking the towel off my neck to wipe my face. A water bottle appeared before me, and I took it, gratefully sipping on it as I looked up. Micah and Brayden were standing shoulder to shoulder in the tiny airplane bathroom, worry pinching their faces.

"I didn't try to crash the plane, did I?" I asked.

They both seemed to relax at my question. "No, Angel, you didn't try to crash the plane. Truthfully, we wouldn't have known anything was happening if it wasn't for Parker telling us when he couldn't wake you no matter what he did."

"Why do I feel no nauseous?" I grumbled.

"If these assholes would let me through, I could fix that," Parker snapped.

Brayden and Micah stepped out of the bathroom but stood right by the door, keeping an eye on what was going on.

"Sorry, Trouble. When I couldn't wake you, I tried to trick your body into thinking you were going to be sick so it would wake up. Obviously it didn't work, so now I have to turn it off," Parker explained, placing his hands on either side of my head.

A warmth flowed through my body, and in an instant my nausea was gone. The headache stuck around, but other than that I was back to normal.

"Thank you," I whispered before I leaned my head against his chest and closed my eyes.

"Hey, hey, no going back to sleep. You have to tell us what just happened," Parker said, pulling me away from him.

"Can we talk about this not in the bathroom?" I asked with a grin pulling at my lips.

Parker shook his head, helping me to my feet, and we headed back out to the main seating area. They were serious about this no sleeping thing. Brayden wrapped his arm around me and led me over to the couch where I snuggled in next to him, feeling a bone-chilling cold from my encounter with the Dark Lord.

A hand rested on my knee, drawing my attention forward. Hudson was squatting in front of me, his blue eyes filled with worry. "What happened? This seems different from what you told us about the other attacks."

"The Dark Lord decided that we needed to have another chat. He knew that Parker was trying to get me out of the dream, but he wasn't worried because Parker wasn't strong enough," I sighed.

Brayden's arm tightened around my shoulders as his body tensed at my words. "What did he want?"

"He wanted me to give myself to him with the promise he would spare all of you from what he has planned for the world," I answered. "I told him to fuck off."

Micah snorted at that, causing me to look at him and the

glint of humor in his eyes. "Really, you stood there and told the Dark Lord to fuck off?"

Frowning at him, I turned and snuggled back against Brayden, refusing to look at him.

"Is there anything else that he said? I can't imagine he would take that response very well," Hudson pushed, bringing us back to the topic at hand.

"He told me that whatever happens from here on out is on me because I could have stopped it, but nothing specific," I said, my gaze falling to my hands, unable to look at them.

A hand tucked under my chin, and Hudson brought my gaze up to meet his eyes. "Lailah, you did the right thing. You can never trust what any demon tells you, let alone the Dark Lord himself. He is the king of lies and manipulation. Whatever happens going forward, we will deal with together. That's why the angels brought the Elementi into existence in the first place. No one person would be able to do this all alone."

I leaned forward and wrapped my arms around Hudson's neck, hugging him to me as he pulled me close. As much as Brayden grounded me, the logic Hudson provided always soothed my fears.

"If you guys won't let me sleep, can we watch a movie?" I asked into Hudson's neck.

His body shook with a soft chuckle. "I think we can do that."

CHAPTER 5

LAILAH

Thankfully, the rest of the flight was uneventful, and we all relaxed as we watched *How to Lose a Guy in 10 Days* for the last few hours of the trip. When we landed, it was early evening, the sun still bright enough to see my surroundings. The airport was literally right on the water... like, if the plane didn't stop in time, we would end up in the sea. It was a stunning teal-blue color though, with soft ripples as far as the eye could see. For someone who never planned on traveling much in her life, this was an experience.

Since we flew in on a private plane, we had a separate office that we had to exit through, and I got yet another stamp in my passport. Out front was a black limousine with a driver standing, holding a sign that said "Lacy Pharmaceuticals, Inc." Hudson led the way over to the limo as the driver opened the back door for us all to slide in.

"Okay, is this going to be a thing with all of your families? Do you all have limos and drivers to take you everywhere?" I teased once we were all in.

"Nah, limos aren't my dad's style. We're a stretch Hummer

kind of family," Parker said with a wink, making it hard to tell if he was serious or not.

Hudson nudged me with his shoulder. "This is not normal for us, either. I think it's the only vehicle they had that would fit all of us."

"My father would expect us to find our own way," Jay stated, looking out the window at the sights. Truthfully, with the little that I knew of his father, that didn't surprise me one bit.

The driver took us up into the hills, maneuvering the narrow streets with an ease that I would never understand. I was beyond thankful that I had the guys with me for these adventures, because I would have been lost beyond hope. Finally, we pulled onto a long gravel drive that ended with a circle, providing a way back out. The front of the villa was a breathtaking piece of history sitting right before me on the edge of a cliff overlooking the town and the water below.

The villa was made out of white stone with terraces on each of the two upper levels, the railings made out of wrought iron. Once out of the limo and standing at the bottom of the stone steps leading up to the front door, I just gaped in awe at the wooden French doors inlaid with beautiful stained glass. Looking to my right, I saw a large swimming pool with a garden just beyond it. As I gawked, Hudson knocked on the door, and moments later it was opened by a small older woman with wispy gray hair piled up on the top of her head.

"Hudson, *mon coeur*! I am so happy to have you home," she cried, reaching up to grab his face and kiss both his cheeks. "*Tu es parti depuis trop longtemps.* Come in, come in."

"Juliette, it is good to see you too. Are Grace and Ben home?" Hudson asked as he let the woman tug him into the house.

"*Oui, oui,* they are home for Christmas break," Juliette said, waving off his question as she turned to take the rest of us in. "So, these are your friends your *mère* told me to expect, *mon coeur*?"

"Yes, this is Lailah, Brayden, Micah, Parker, and Jay. We all go to school together at Ryevick University. Guys, this is Juliette. She has been looking after me since Father and I moved to France," Hudson shared, giving the older woman a soft, sweet smile.

"Oh, so you must have many embarrassing stories to tell us?" I grinned, excited to learn more about Hudson.

As much as I loved how stable and even Hudson is, it caused me to feel like I didn't really know who he truly was. No one could be as perfect as he seemed to be; there had to be something in his past to make him seem more human like the rest of us.

"*Les enfants, viennet ici!*" Juliette called up the staircase.

By the sound of feet coming down the stairs, I guess she had called for Hudson's siblings. Sure enough, a young man with olive skin, dark, thick hair, and chocolate-colored eyes appeared. He was striking to look at, and there was almost nothing of Hudson's father in him. Following on his heels was a tall, willowy girl with a bouncing chin-length bob of honey brown hair. Her blue eyes looked at us curiously as they came to stand at the bottom of the stairs.

"Ben, Grace, these are my friends from school," Hudson said as they bobbed their heads in greeting to us.

"*Coucou,*" Grace said, waving at us with a smile.

"*Bonjour.*" Ben's voice was so soft I almost missed what he was saying.

"Did Mother tell you guys that we will be around for a few days?" Hudson asked.

"No, but Mère has not been home much the past few days," Grace said, shrugging her shoulders. "It will be nice to have some people in the house for a change."

"Oh! What am I, you ungrateful child?" Juliette scoffed. "Now show them where they will be staying so this old woman doesn't need to climb the stairs while I'm trying to make dinner."

Grace blushed as she gestured for us to follow her with her head. "All the guest rooms are on the third floor, but some of you are going to have to share. We only have three."

I don't think my eyes could have gotten any wider as we made our way through the house. The ground floor was all white marble that flowed onto the stairs with a wrought iron banister that curved up to the second floor. The whole house was painted in creams and white, making it seem so regal. It wasn't a place you would call "homey," like Brayden's home. This was filled with antique furniture and brocade fabrics, crystal chandeliers hanging in the halls. I felt like I was on some period movie set. Taking us up another flight, we ended up in a small sitting area with two large glass doors that opened onto a cobblestone terrace.

Grace gestured down the hall to the left. "Feel free to pick what works for you. There's a bathroom at the end of the hall."

Not needing more encouragement, I wandered down the hall, opening the first door to find a room with two twin beds on either side. It was light and cheerful with lots of windows, making the small space seem bigger. Moving to the next room, I found what I was guessing was a full-size bed with a tufted couch against one wall and a set of doors to a small balcony. Going across the hall, I found the room I was going to be staying in. Framed in a set of arched French doors was a view of the water. The room was the most inviting, even if it was the gaudiest with gold accents and warm-toned hardwood floors.

"So, how are we going to decide who gets to bunk with Lailah for the next few days?" Parker asked from right behind me, making me jump.

"It only makes sense that I do because we are bonded," Brayden said, sitting on the bed.

Parker crossed his arms, looking down at him. "Nope, not

gonna happen this time. The only reason we didn't argue before was that none of us had even kissed her yet. Now that that's changed, we need to come up with a new plan. I want my time with her."

"Hey, Parker, your man whore is showing," Micah growled.

Rounding on him, Parker raised a fist, but before he could land the blow, Jay intercepted and twisted his arm behind his back. "Lailah is not a bone to fight over. She can decide who she spends time with, and we will all listen to her choice, giving her the respect she deserves."

I felt my brows climb in my surprise at Jay's outburst. When he felt that Parker was back under control, he let him go and stepped away but kept a wary eye on him.

"If I might offer a suggestion," Hudson interjected. "If Lailah feels comfortable with this, we could alternate who gets to share the bed. That way no one person gets the privilege over the other."

None of the boys seemed thrilled with the plan, but I wasn't totally opposed. I just wasn't sure that all of them wanted to sleep next to me. Sure, most of us had exchanged a few kisses, but that didn't mean they were ready to be that intimate with me. Nor I them.

"If we cannot agree, then Lailah will have the room to herself and one of you can bunk with me in my room on the second floor," Hudson added when no one said anything.

"I think that will be best," I decided.

Parker looked like he wanted to argue with me, and Brayden looked none too happy, but a grunt from Jay had them keeping their mouths shut.

"Seriously, guys. It's not like I won't be spending all my waking time with you. Is it that big of a deal not to bunk with me?" I asked, not getting why this was such a big deal.

Jay walked up to me and cupped my chin in his hand. "You do not have to justify your choice, Lailah. I will make sure that it is respected." Kissing me gently on the forehead, he headed out of my room and down the hall.

"I call the single room!" Micah called out as he headed off after Jay.

"Too late," was all I heard, followed by Micah swearing.

I couldn't help but giggle at them and how much they sounded like my own brothers back home.

"Who's gonna room with me?" Hudson asked, looking at Parker and Brayden.

"Somehow, I think it would be best for me to room with Micah." Brayden grinned. "I'm not sure Parker would live through the night if he was alone with Micah that long."

Parker scrunched up his face in disgust. "Like I was ever going to share a room with him. I would sleep on the couch in Jay's room before I did that."

"Come on, let's leave Lailah to get settled before we all head down for dinner," Hudson said, ushering out the guys. "After dinner, we can head out to the lab and find out what my parents have for us so far. It'd also be good to check in with Beth to make sure she is in the loop on all that's happening."

Hearing him talk about Beth made me realize I should call Cami. Things had been so crazy, I hadn't called her back after the party like I promised. Grabbing my backpack, I tossed it on the bed and pulled out my phone, then wandered out on the balcony. I found a wicker bench with seat cushions and settled down, hitting the video call button. After a few rings, Cami's face popped up, her bright green eyes wide with excitement. I'd forgotten that she dyed her short, funky hair neon-green—her favorite color.

"LALA! You beautiful bitch you, why didn't you call me sooner?" Cami demanded. "How did last night go? Did they all drool over your bangin' body in that dress? Oh, did they have any dancing? Come on girl, stop stalling and spill the tea!"

"The guys loved the dress. You should have seen them all—

even Micah was impressed," I shared, smiling as she rolled her eyes. "There was no dancing, but it really wasn't that type of party. Much too posh for that."

"Well, that's boring. What did you end up doing all night?" Cami asked. Something must have shown on my face, because she sat up in bed and her face turned more serious. "Lala, tell me what happened."

Taking a deep breath, I told her the whole story about Tabitha and the showdown we had outside in the hotel garden. She waited patiently until I was finished and explained how I was now in France at Hudson's mom's house.

"Babe, we really need to work on this communication thing between us. Now I know why Beth has been MIA for the last day or so. Damn it, I should have been there with you instead of here safe in my bedroom," Cami grumbled.

Fear shot through me at the thought of Cami in danger. "Absolutely not! I would have lost my shit if anything happened to you."

"Aww, you're so upset you're even swearing. I feel so special," Cami teased.

"I'm being serious here. The only reason we survived is because we are the Elementi Warriors. A normal human would have been destroyed," I snapped.

Cami blinked at me, surprised at my outburst. "That battle really scared you, didn't it?"

It was then that I realized I had been holding it together for the guys, but now, talking to my best friend, I couldn't pretend anymore.

"You have no idea how terrified I was that I would lose one of them. Tabitha was so much stronger than I could have imagined, and she's only the tip of the iceberg. The Dark Lord is talking to me in my dreams, taunting me, and I'm afraid one of these times I'm not going to survive the encounter," I sobbed, finally letting my emotions out. "What if he's right and the evil inside of me is growing? Could I become a danger to the people I care about? The guys act like nothing's wrong, but I know the truth."

"Shut the fuck up, Lailah," Cami barked at me.

Stunned, my mouth snapped shut, and I sat there silently.

"You listen to me, and you listen good. I get you are scared and this battle showed you the dark side of being part of the Elementi and what it could mean for you and the guys in the future. Now, what I want you to do is take that fear and use it, learn from it. You're going to be starting your studies when you get back, and now you see just how much you need to catch up on if you want to protect those around you. Don't let your fear chase you away from the darkness. Own that it's a part of you and do something about it!"

"You're right," I murmured, feeling thoroughly chastised.

"Damn right I am! Now pull your shit together, investigate what that bitch-ass demon lord is up to, and enjoy being in France for Christmas surrounded by your men," Cami commanded.

Wiping the remnants of my tears off my cheeks, I gave her a smile. "Yes ma'am."

"I love the fuck out of you babe, but sometimes you get lost in that beautiful head of yours," Cami said with a smirk. "Now hang up with me and go enjoy your night."

"Love you, talk later," I said, giving her a wave and hanging up the call.

CHAPTER 6

HUDSON

Dinner was a quiet affair, but it always had been growing up in this house. Mother always had lots on her mind, and our "chatter" would give her a headache. So now all of us were conditioned to eat in silence, and the others seemed to follow our lead. When I was young, Father would join us, but as I got older, he stayed late at the office more than he was home. He tried doing what he could to keep the fights from happening in front of my siblings, but Mother's voice would carry through the house. That's what led to him moving out before everything was finalized.

I know many kids feel responsible or part of the cause for their parents' divorce, but I was raised far too rational to believe that. My mother and father were better off not being married. If they had stayed together just for us kids, it would have done more harm than good. So I don't resent them having to do what they needed to, dissolving their marriage.

Back in the limo once again, we headed to the lab. I stared out the window at the place I spent most of my early childhood. A hand twining its fingers with mine caused me to glance down to see Lailah's crystal blue eyes looking up at me, worried.

"Everything okay?" she asked in a quiet voice.

"I haven't been back here in many years. The only reason I decided to come back was because my father asked me to," I explained.

Just because I didn't show my feelings outwardly didn't mean once I was away from my parents I didn't see how toxic it was. I loved my father deeply, and on his own he was the man I grew up admiring, kind and logical. When he was around Isabelle, though, it was like he changed into a different person, more spiteful.

"When I came into my powers at thirteen, Mother sent me away to be trained at an Elementi facility," I continued when Lailah didn't say anything. "That's where I completed high school. During the summers, the other four would join me, and that is where we started training together. My mother didn't want Ben and Grace to know anything about the Elementi. Part of me thinks that is what started to cause their marriage to crumble."

To my surprise, all Lailah did was rest her head on my shoulder and hug my arm, offering her support. So many times when I tell people my story, they want to fix things or help me find resolution to my situation, but here she was, giving me what I needed most.

"I talked to Beth before dinner," Brayden announced, and all eyes turned to him. "She is aware of the situation since my parents and Hudson's dad reached out to her. On their end, they are combing through the video footage, trying to place a timeline on when the serum went missing. It'll give us a better pool of people to talk to based on who was in the building at the time."

Micah grunted. "What makes them think it will be that easy? Demons are the best at going unnoticed; it's how they survive this world."

"True, but if Tabitha was correct and it was a member of the

Dark Lord's army, then it would be a human and not a demon," I countered.

"Seriously, Hudson? Why would we believe anything that came out of that woman's mouth? You saw the demonic energy she had inside her. How is that much different than being possessed by a mid-level demon?" Micah challenged. "No, we need to do what Lailah said this morning and go into it without any preconceived notions."

Lailah sat up, grinning at Micah. "Hold on, Micah—did you just say that you agree with me about something?"

Micah rolled his eyes at her, but I could see the glint of humor in his eyes. "I wouldn't go that far, Cookie Monster."

I turned to Jay, who, as always, was watching what was going on around him with a calculating gaze. When he saw me watching him, he raised a questioning brow.

"What do you know of the Dark Lord's army? Your father mentioned that he had been keeping an eye on their activity," I asked, quieting the others.

"We don't know much as my father said. Every time we find the location of one of their hideouts, it's been abandoned. They don't behave like other armies or even terrorist cells; there is no communication or paper trail to follow," Jay explained.

I nodded, leaning my head back against the window, closing my eyes as I rolled that information around my brain.

* * *

"Monsieur Lacy, I presume?" the woman at the reception desk asked as we entered the large building that housed the lab and offices of Lacy Pharmaceuticals.

Walking out from behind the desk, I noticed that she wasn't much older than I was. She had bright red hair that fell around her shoulders, contrasting the emerald-green button-down she had on. As she approached, she had a smirk on her lips as she let her eyes rove over me. Flipping her hair over one shoulder, she revealed that a few too many buttons were undone, and the black lace of her bra peeked out.

"I'm Sophie. I work in the Department of Human Resources, and your father thought I could be of use to you getting whatever information you needed," Sophie purred as she leaned in to greet me.

Lailah stepped in between us, holding out her hand. "It's so nice to meet you, Sophie. I'm Lailah." Sophie tried to hide her distaste for Lailah—poorly—as she shook her hand. "Speaking of Mr. Lacy, where might we find him? There is some information we can only get from him directly, something I don't think we could find in the HR department."

Someone behind me coughed, trying to cover their laughter, and I myself had a hard time keeping a smile off my face. To see Lailah so protective of me warmed my heart in a way I don't think anyone else could. My golden ray of sunshine didn't need to worry about a woman like this distracting me from her. The only light I needed in my life was standing guard over me like the Knight she was.

"But of course," Sophie said. Walking back to the desk, she grabbed lanyards that had security passes hanging from them.

When she tried to place the lanyard over my head, I grabbed her wrist, stopping her. Gently, I removed the lanyard from her hand and put it around my own neck.

"You will need these to get anywhere in the building. Monsieur Lacy gave you full access to the labs; there is nowhere that is off limits to you and your friends in that section. I shall wait here when you are ready to deal with any of the employee matters. If you wish to enter the office side of the building, I will need to escort you personally, per Mademoiselle Dupont's wishes," Sophie said, giving Lailah a lofty look.

"Tonight we will just be in the labs, so you may leave for the evening," I stated, giving Sophie a sharp look.

"*Tres bien*," Sophie huffed with another flick of her hair. "I shall see you in the morning."

Not wanting to deal with her any longer, I headed for the door I knew would lead us into the labs, swiping the key card over the sensor. Once the door was shut behind us all, Parker burst out laughing.

"Oh man, that was priceless!" He slapped me on the back much harder than I would have liked. "Who knew you had game, Hudson? That woman wanted a piece of you, bad. And let's not forget how Trouble almost clawed her face off when she tried to make a move on you."

Lailah shoved Parker, scowling at him. "It's not funny, Parker."

"You're right, it wasn't funny. That shit right there was hilarious," Parker chuckled, grabbing Lailah in a headlock as she tried and failed to attack him. "Aw, come on. The jealous side of you is adorable. You're just going to have to own that shit."

"Fuck off," Lailah grumbled.

We all laughed at that, and I had to agree with Parker. It was cute to see her so protective over me.

CHAPTER 7

LAILAH

As we all walked down the hall following Hudson, Parker refused to let go of my hand. One side of the hall was full of glass walls showing clean rooms, and the other side had labs filled with equipment that I had no idea what they did. It reminded me of the days I'd worked with Hudson at school for extra credit, only far more high tech.

At the end of the hall, a large wooden door with a nameplate on it told me we had arrived at his father's office. Without knocking, Hudson walked in, holding the door open for us. It was an interesting combination of workspace—with microscopes, sample trays, veils, and other lab paraphernalia—and a typical office with a large desk.

Mr. Lacy was seated at said desk, the blue glow of his computer reflecting off his glasses. He didn't even look up when we entered the room, just kept typing away at whatever he was working on. Papers were strewn across his desk, and some even fell onto the floor. From the little I knew of the man, I hazarded a guess that this was very uncharacteristic of him.

"Father," Hudson called out, causing his father's head to shoot over to our direction.

His immediate frown relaxed once he saw who it was that had interrupted him. "Ah, you've all made it."

Pushing away from his desk, he walked over to us, gesturing for us to take a seat on the leather couch he had in the office. From the looks of it, I could tell he'd spent a few nights sleeping on it.

"You didn't have any trouble getting your security passes, did you?" he asked, combing his fingers through his hair.

Seeing Hudson's dad this ruffled told me that this was turning into a bigger deal than we originally thought.

"No problem, Sophie was very helpful," I answered, unable to keep the bite out of my voice.

Mr. Lacy nodded his head as he leaned against the front of his desk, rubbing his chin, lost in thought.

"Father, why don't you tell us what you've found out so far," Hudson directed, seeing that we wouldn't get anywhere fast.

This seemed to perk Mr. Lacy up, as he started digging through the files and papers, grabbing a few and muttering to himself. "Where did that report go? Ah! Here it is," he exclaimed, swooping down to grab a few sheets off the floor.

"Lailah, since you asked me about the properties of demon venom, I have my specialty Elementi section running tests. We don't have a ton of new information, but we have more than we did this morning. As things progress, I will have them combine what we know with the Day-Brite serum so we will have a better clue as to what the effects will be," he said, handing over all the findings to me.

With a quick glance at the information before me, I knew there was no way I would be able to tell what it said. I passed it to Hudson, hoping he could make heads or tails out of it.

"The first thing we discovered is that demon venom is able to change its makeup so that the body won't reject it. It shifts itself into something that resembles your DNA. If you know to look for it, you can see the small differences, but it's close enough that if you went to the doctor and got a blood draw, no one would see anything wrong," Mr. Lacy continued.

"So, the blood test we do at the school will be useless," Brayden said, his face showing his shock.

I frowned, not understanding. "What does that have to do with anything? I thought it was a way to search for Synergy?"

"No, originally we did it so that if a demon-possessed person tried to enroll in the school, we would know. As we have experienced, the wards are great when they work, but it's always wise to have a backup system," Brayden explained.

"That's not even the worst of it," Mr. Lacy announced.

"Sure, why not, because that wasn't a big enough problem to deal with," Parker muttered.

Micah reached over and slapped him upside the head, glaring at him.

"Lailah, you said that you are demon-tainted, correct? What are the side effects you have experienced?" Mr. Lacy asked, his eyes softening as he looked at me.

My stomach dropped as I remembered what the Dark Lord said to me about it spreading in me. "Please just tell me what you found out," I whispered, dropping my gaze to my hands.

"Know that this is only a preliminary finding; it's not to say that this happens every time and in all situations. This sample was not treated like yours was, it was left in its pure form." Hearing that didn't make me feel better. "We are finding that the venom can change existing cells of the body as well. It slowly alters your essence into something else."

I blinked rapidly, trying to keep tears from falling as I absorbed the news. It seemed that the Dark Lord wasn't lying about everything. Makes sense, though. It was an easy way for me to feel defeated and to believe that giving into him was the only way to survive.

Well, I would rather kill myself than end up as a weapon used to destroy everything around me.

Clearing my throat, I looked up, meeting Chadwick's gaze and seeing the pity there. Parker wrapped his arm around my shoulders, and Hudson placed a hand on my knee, giving me a reassuring squeeze. "Thank you for letting me know the possibility of what might happen, but let's not let it distract us from dealing with the reason we are here."

Something akin to admiration now showed in his eyes, and with a nod of his head, he shifted to grab another file off his desk. "I pulled all the reports we have on tests conducted on the Day-Brite serum to see if I could find anything new now that I'm looking at it from a different perspective. It seems that in allowing the brain to be open to more information, it also has made it more susceptible to persuasion. Not only in thinking, but personality as well. When memory loss happens, it can make the person more irritable, short-tempered, and mean. That was one area we wanted to help improve by boosting the limbic system."

"Sorry sir, but not all of us are science nerds and understand what you're saying," Micah interjected.

"Oh, thank god someone said it. I thought I was gonna need the dummy's book version there for a second," Parker muttered under his breath.

Mr. Lacy smiled. "Sorry, I forget that I'm not talking to colleagues. The drug by itself is meant to help the brain still retain information while keeping the mood stable. If it was tampered with, it could make the brain more suggestible or even alter emotions—positively or negatively."

"Okay, let me see if I understand," I ventured, leaning forward, elbows on my knees. "In an average human, it would help to prevent them from becoming so volatile, but if it was used on someone who might be mentally ill or unstable for another reason, it could amplify those emotions."

"Yes. When you look at it as a weapon and not as a drug to help someone, it opens up a whole realm of possibilities. Add in the demon venom, and we have people who could have their whole personality rewritten into the perfect soldier that is extremely hard to detect. What really worries me is that even if we have all this information, we don't know where or why he is building this army now." Mr. Lacy sighed as he rubbed his forehead.

I stood up and gently placed my hand on his arm. "We will take this one step at a time. You didn't sleep very well last night, and you were up before the sun today. My guess is that you haven't taken a break or really eaten anything with the amount you've gotten done. Go home. We will be back tomorrow, and we can look at this with fresh eyes. We are here to help in any way we can, starting with the personnel."

Mr. Lacy covered my hand with his and gave me a soft smile. "I think you're right. A tired brain is a careless brain, and we need to be sharp. Our enemy is sly, so we must be up to the task of searching it out wherever it might be hiding. Come, I'll walk you out since you will need to leave your security passes here. Last thing we need is for one of those to fall into the wrong hands."

Taking off our passes, we left them on his desk as he grabbed his suit jacket and briefcase. As we headed out of the office, Hudson stopped me and pulled me into a hug.

"Thank you, Sunshine. He wouldn't have listened to me if I'd asked," Hudson said into my hair.

Wrapping my arms around him, I held onto him tightly. "He's your family, Hudson. Therefore, he's family to me, too."

As I snuggled into bed, I stared out the glass French doors at the sea alight with the moon's glow. Even though it had only been a little over a month since Brayden and I bonded, it was hard to sleep by myself. It didn't help that my brain wanted to go over every detail that Mr. Lacy told us about the demon venom and the serum.

Synergy. The fabled sixth element that was supposed to be the change in the tide. What good was I to anyone if I turned out to destroy the world instead of save it, all because of demon venom? Could I actually be changed into something else? Was the Dark Lord right? Seriously, what could a bunch of kids do against the darkest evil that roamed the world?

In our conversation tonight, we'd just touched the tip of the iceberg of what could happen with the serum, let alone what the serum mixed with demon venom could do. Was it really that easy to infect someone with demon venom and let it run its course? How many people had they turned this way?

In the quiet of the night, alone in this room, I let myself break down. I'd tried so hard not to let what the Dark Lord said get to me, but it's harder when you have the facts laid out in front of you. These were the top researchers and scientific minds the Elementi had working on this; I couldn't just dismiss what they found... could I?

I felt my tears roll down my cheeks onto the pillow, trying to keep my sobs quiet. I didn't know anyone was in my room until I felt the mattress sink under their weight. I lifted my head and found Jay looking down at me, his brow creased with concern. The moment he saw my tears, he lifted the blankets and crawled into the bed, pulling me against his bare chest. Wrapped up in his strong hold, I felt shielded from the world and all the darkness I knew was lurking out there.

My sobs shook my body as I gripped his shoulders, my face buried in his neck. Gently, he combed his fingers through my hair, helping me to calm and soothing my gasping breaths. When I was finally all cried out, he pulled me away from him and wiped the tears off my face with the sheet. He searched my face, and I felt like I was laid bare to him, my emotions raw. Still silent, he pulled me back to him, kissing my forehead, and tucked me under his chin as he wrapped us both up in the blanket, letting out a heavy sigh that caused me to do the same. Listening to the steady beat of his heart and the even breaths he took, I was finally able to drift off to sleep, knowing I was completely safe.

CHAPTER 8
LAILAH

As the warm sunlight filtered into the room, I scrunched up my face and tried to roll over, but I was stopped as arms tightened their hold on me. I tried to open my eyes, but they were gritty from crying last night. Pulling an arm out from under Jay's weight—he was half laying on me—I rubbed my eyes. One of Jay's hands was still in my hair, and it tightened as I once again tried to move out from under him.

"Jay, you need to let me up. We have a lot to do," I whispered as he nuzzled into my neck.

"No."

I couldn't hold back the smile at how cuddly Jay was. He wasn't one who needed much physical affection, being more of a man of action and service. This was a change, and one that I wasn't mad at. I let my hand trail down his back, tracing over his muscles and a few of the tattoos that he had draping over his shoulder. His muscles shifted under my touch, followed by his lips brushing along my neck, sending tingles through my body.

Using his hold in my hair, he pulled my head to the side, giving him better access to my throat. He let his teeth skim along the column of skin, causing me to gasp and dig my nails into his back. This made Jay growl into my neck, nipping at me before he shifted so we were both on our sides with him behind me.

"We don't have time to play that game, beautiful," Jay rasped in my ear, his voice still thick with sleep. "But I can take care of you another way."

Catching up both my hands, he trapped them to my chest, holding me tight against him. Slowly, he dragged his teeth on the outside shell of my ear before he bit down on the lobe. I arched against him, rubbing my ass along his rigid dick, which let me know he was as into this as I was. Jay let his free hand roam over my bare stomach, my shirt having ridden up in the night. Slowly, he moved lower until he let a finger dip just under the elastic of my sleep pants. Squirming, I tried to urge his hand lower, but he withdrew it, letting it rest just under my boobs.

"You have to keep still or I'll stop," Jay threatened, the command clear in his voice.

Letting out a whimper, I surrendered to his hold, and after a moment he began his slow journey back down. This time he let two fingers skim under the elastic, letting them run along the top of my pelvis—so close, yet so far. It took everything in me to hold still and not thrust up into his hand. Distracting me, he started kissing along my neck again as he moved further down my leg, pushing my sleep pants down. Once my pants were off, by some magic he'd performed with one hand, he lifted my right leg and settled it over top of his, leaving me exposed if anyone walked into the room.

My heart started beating faster with the fear—and oddly, the excitement—of us doing this and getting away with it. I knew that Jay, in particular, enjoyed watching, but I wasn't sure if the other men in my life shared that proclivity. I sucked in a sharp breath as Jay's fingers trailed along the inside of my thigh until he reached where it met the rest of my body. He hadn't even touched my clit or anywhere near my vagina, and I knew it was drenched with anticipation. Catching me off guard, he glided his finger along the seam, making me cry out at the shock.

"If you don't want them seeing this, then I might suggest keeping your voice down," Jay purred against my jaw.

Swallowing down another moan, I couldn't help but arch as he circled my clit with his finger. I almost wept as he pulled his hand away in punishment for my actions.

"Jay, please," I begged, turning my face slightly to look at him. "I'm sorry, I won't move. Please just let me come."

A predatory glint showed in Jay's silver eyes as he plunged two fingers into me, muffling my scream with his mouth. Everything about Jay in this moment was commanding—he set the pace, and I was only allowed to follow. Using his thumb, he applied pressure to my nub as he worked his fingers in and out of me. I desperately wanted to pull my arms out of his hold so I could wrap them around his neck, but there wasn't a chance in hell I was going to let him stop.

His kiss was harsh as he explored my mouth, shifting me so he was slightly more on top of me. Never had I been so at someone's mercy and reveled in it. There wasn't a fear in my mind other than he might stop before I completed, but all I had to do was let him take care of me as he always did. My orgasm blindsided me as it rocketed through my body, but Jay didn't stop. Instead he sped up and pushed through the tightening of my walls. Moments after the first one, he slipped a third finger in, and a second release was barreling down on me.

There was no way I could hold still as I shattered apart under his touch. My body acted of its own will, curling up on itself as Jay forced every ounce of mind-blowing pleasure out of my body. Finally, he slowed, sending shockwaves through my body each time he flicked his fingers before he removed them. Languid and panting, I watched as he took those three fingers and placed them in his mouth, holding my gaze as he did. If I hadn't been wrung out, I would have demanded another round right then and there, but I wasn't sure I could move yet.

Gently, Jay rolled me so I was facing him, and he gently massaged my body, helping me come down from my high. He cupped my face with both his hands and placed gentle kisses on my forehead, nose, lips. "You listened well, my beautiful girl."

I blushed at his words as they filled me with such warmth I couldn't help but smile. A door somewhere along the hall slammed, letting us know that someone else was awake and I might not have been as quiet as I'd thought I'd been.

No one made any comment or even asked about what they might have heard during breakfast. Granted, Ben and Grace were eating with us, so that would have been embarrassing. Just when we finished our meal, I heard heels clicking on the marble floors, announcing Isabelle's presence. She quickly entered the dining room and stopped as she was putting on her watch, looking surprised to find us all there.

Her thick, dark hair had a slight wave and was shaped into a trendy short style. Defining brows shaped her dark brown eyes, and her full lips were pursed in displeasure. Quickly, she regained her composure and let her gaze sweep the table until she landed on Hudson.

"Why aren't you at the office?" Isabelle demanded. "It's almost nine. I was expecting you to be there early so you didn't disturb us during business hours."

As she spoke, I watched Hudson become more rigid and his expression slip into the cool, detached look he'd always worn when I first met him. "I wasn't aware of this, Mother. We stopped by last night, and Sophie didn't share that information with us."

Isabelle's eyebrows rose. "Why would she? I explained this

all to your father. He should have told you my expectations. Things need to carry on like normal. We can't let Chadwick's blunder tarnish the reputation I have built for this company."

Hudson told me that his parents didn't get along, but the things that were coming out of this woman's mouth were shocking me. Coming from a home with loving parents, I had no experience dealing with a situation like this, and I was afraid to say something and make it worse.

"We were just going to head that way. You have my promise that we will do all we can not to disrupt things. There is still more that we need to do in the labs, so we can deal with that today and get an early start tomorrow, if you would like," Hudson suggested, proving just how skilled he was at dealing with his mother.

Isabelle sniffed and pulled on her suit jacket. "What I would like is for this never to have happened. This is what you get for working with friends. It's better to keep things professional on all levels. That woman is losing her mind. Why would he think she was a safe project partner? I'll bet she's the one who had it stolen. Paranoia is strong in the early stages of dementia."

As Isabelle's words registered in my brain, my temper flared. I moved to get out of my seat, but Brayden grabbed my arm. Looking at him, shocked, he just gave a quick shake of his head. Frowning, I couldn't understand why we weren't more upset about this. She was trash, talking badly about his mother, who wasn't at fault for any of this.

"Ben, Grace, I expect you to be working on those projects for next semester. These two weeks are not a time for you to get sloppy if you want to get into Harvard next year, Grace. Ben, I talked to the school board at MIT, and there is still hope for you if you find the will to apply yourself this semester. Two Bs— honestly, how could you have let your grades slip like that?" Isabelle huffed, shaking her head as she grabbed her purse and marched out of the room.

I waited long enough to hear the door close and for the house to fall silent before I let out what I'd been holding back. "What the hell was that?"

Hudson dropped his head into his hand, and his siblings shifted in their chairs as if they wanted to be anywhere but here. I couldn't blame them. If I had just had my mother verbally smack my hands with a ruler in front of strangers, I would have been mortified too.

"Well, now you have all met our mother," Hudson said, lifting his head back up, but he still wouldn't look me in the eyes.

I could see right away that he needed to stay far away from that woman or all the progress I'd made with him opening up to me would be lost. Never had I imagined a mother being so cold to her kids.

"Let's go. We don't want to waste any more time getting this done," Micah said, pushing back from the table. It didn't surprise me to see the anger shining in his eyes. Adriana was as much a mother to him as to Brayden.

This time, an SUV came to get us, and we all piled in as we headed back to the lab. Sophie was nowhere in sight when we got there, making me feel better. A lab assistant came out in an all-white jumpsuit with a hair net on, handing us out passes.

"Monsieur Lacy asked me to escort you," the lab tech said, waving at us to follow.

We all looked at each other, then Parker shrugged and headed off after the guy.

CHAPTER 9
LAILAH

I could see why Mr. Lacy wanted us to have a guide, because there is no way we would have found this specific lab tucked away. It was even in a separate wing with retinal scanners off the main lab section. Since we are in the Elementi database, we didn't need to add our information and just needed the lab security cards to get in, but again—only if we found it.

"As you can see, this is the lab set aside to work on any and all Elementi-specific needs. We have been able to recreate the serum and combine it with the demon venom to see what the reaction will be," Lewis explained, stepping over to a counter that had a large screen hanging on the wall.

He typed in the passcode, and information sprang onto the screen. If I had any clue as to what it said, I might have had more of a reaction, but as it stood, we all waited silently. Hudson stepped forward, adjusting his glasses as he scanned the information.

Hudson turned sharply on Lewis. "Are you sure? Can it be reversed?"

"No, it is permanent."

"Um, anyone care to share with the rest of the group what we should be freaking out about?" Parker interjected.

They both looked back at us with grim looks on their faces. "This serum with the added venom turns them into the perfect host for a mid-level demon, but because they don't need to fight the host, they don't deteriorate the same way," Lewis answered.

"You can't tell that from computer scenarios," Micah snapped. "This is all speculation—right?"

Lewis grabbed a remote and clicked the center button, and the sound of something being pulled back whirred behind us. Glancing over my shoulder, I saw a man strapped to a table, writhing and spitting as he yelled. The glass must have been soundproof, because I couldn't hear a thing.

"Okay, a demon-possessed man behind curtain number one is something I would have expected from Jay's dad, not yours, Hudson," Parker stage whispered.

Registering what Parker just said, I gasped. "That man is possessed by a *demon*?"

"Yes, *mademoiselle*, we have a sacred circle around him to keep him from exiting the body, so he is trapped at the moment. There is nothing to fear from it," Lewis informed me, misunderstanding my shock.

Anger spiked as I connected a few things. Marching up to Lewis, I got right in his face.

"Did you give him the serum and then let him get possessed before it was stolen, or did you summon a demon and trap him in that poor man's body so you could study it?" I demanded.

Lewis looked at me without batting an eye. "Both, I guess you could say. He was one of our human test subjects, the only one to have been given the serum before it was taken. Once the serum was taken, we then suggested he read an incantation as a test to see how his recall skills were doing. It so happened that he managed to summon a demon and was possessed by it."

"You are part of the Elementi. How could you have done that? It's wrong." I yelled.

"That is where you are wrong. I am not part of the Elementi, just hired by them. We are not bound by the same rules as the inducted Elementi. They need us to work in the gray areas. If we do not, then we are left at a disadvantage when fighting the demons," Lewis said to me, his face reserved and eyes dull.

I took a few steps back and scoffed. "You can't even see how wrong this really is anymore, can you?"

Glancing at the others, I saw the same look of disgust on their faces. I let out a breath, relieved to know they didn't agree with what was happening here.

"Open the room. I want to talk to the man-demon-thing," I ordered, my hands clenched into fists.

"*Mademoiselle,* even if you remove the demon from the man now, he will be incredibly susceptible to having it happen again. His brain pattern has been imprinted with the demon venom, making him a beacon to any roving spirit," Lewis challenged.

Jay stepped up next to me, glaring down at the man. "That is what you meant by permanent."

"Yes. We also don't know how much of the real him is left. Having a demon dwelling in you is sure to speed up the transformation."

"This is nuts," Brayden shouted as he started to pace the floor, running his hands through his hair.

"I did not want to show you for this reason, but your father insisted that I did," grumbled Lewis. "You are all too young to see that this type of work is needed to keep us all safe."

"Enough," Hudson snapped, shocking us all. "Take us to a place that we can have a secure video call with the Elementi HQ at Ryevick."

"Very well." Lewis nodded and ushered us out of the room.

"Please tell me you didn't know about this, Beth," I said to the screen after we explained everything we knew thus far.

Beth looked like she hadn't been able to sleep the last few days. Her usually sleek bob was disheveled, as was the button-down shirt she was wearing. Beth was always particular about a clean and orderly appearance.

"I won't lie to you, Lailah. Did I know about this exact situation—no. Did I know that some of our more dubious work was handed out to contract workers—yes. It is hard to keep every step pure while trying to find a way to deal with demons, I'm afraid. Now, if this matter had been brought to my attention, or if I had even known it was being considered, I would have shut it down completely." Beth sighed, rubbing her forehead. "I need you all to keep in mind that your parents left us out of the loop on this completely; we didn't know anything about it until you did."

"What can we do on our end to help?" Brayden asked, steering the conversation to a safer topic.

Beth looked down at her desk, looking around for something. "So, it looks like we narrowed down the pool of people who were in the building to five hundred and fifty. The tricky part is that with the holiday, not all of these people have been back since. I need you all to find out if they've really just left or if they are taking time off. The HR department likes to keep their information locked away from us if it's not related to Elementi issues."

"Five hundred and fifty isn't that bad with the six of us working on it," Brayden said, relaxing a little.

"Oh, that was just the lab techs. That number didn't include everyone. The total is looking at around two thousand. Honestly, I thought it would be more since they have over seventy thousand people working for them," Beth shared, not noticing the shock we were all in.

Hudson coughed, clearing his throat. "How exactly do you expect us to go through that many employee records?"

"Contact the HR department and they will be able to get you tablets with all the files on them. If Isabelle gives you a hard time, let me know. Chadwick Lacy and the Elementi own the company, not her, a thing she seems to be forgetting. As one of the major shareholders, we can request an employee audit without any suspicion, so there is no harm in giving you what you need. Good luck, and call if you need us to look into anyone further," Beth said with a wave, and the call was cut off.

Parker groaned and flopped onto the table, ever the dramatic one. "Remind me that I never want to be a private eye. There is way too much paperwork."

I smiled, rolling my eyes.

"On the plus side, we get to see Trouble lose her shit when we have to go talk to Sophie again," Parker said, grinning at me.

"Excuse me, I don't know what you're talking about. I did not lose my shit," I huffed.

"You keep telling yourself that, but I can already see you gearing up for another showdown. Here's an idea—just plant one right on his lips if she gets too handsy. Better yet, sit on his lap, staking your claim so she can't miss it," Parker suggested, his eyes wide with excitement.

Micah stood and smacked Parker upside the head as he walked by. "Knock it off. She's not you, all needy and shit."

"Fuck off, man, I know that. I'm just saying she can feel free to claim any one of us in front of another person. I don't know about the rest of you, but I'm not interested in any other woman besides our Trouble," Parker announced, rubbing the back of his head.

Hudson stood from the conference table we had been using. "I think this is a talk we all need to have, but now is not the right time to do that. At the moment, we need to tell my mother that she has to hand over thousands of employee files for us to work on for the next few days."

We all cringed at that thought. If our encounter at breakfast was anything to go by, this wasn't going to be pretty. Already on the office side of the building, it didn't take us long to find Sophie sitting at her desk. Today she was wearing a blood-red wrap dress that had a plunging neckline and might as well have been painted on her body. Her lip color matched the dress, and her thick, wavy hair waterfalled over her shoulder.

"Oh, Monsieur Hudson! I wasn't expecting to see you today. Mademoiselle Dupont said you would be busy in the labs. Although I am very pleased you decided to seek me out," Sophie said, turning in her chair to cross her legs, showing them off.

I thought I could keep my cool, trusting that Hudson wasn't interested in some vapid diva, but the anger coursing through my veins would say otherwise.

"We are looking for Ms. Dupont, could you tell us where to find her?" Brayden asked, trying to pull her attention away from Hudson.

"*Oui.* She is in her office, but she is on an important call and cannot be disturbed. Is there anything I can help you with?" Sophie asked, letting her gaze wander over Brayden.

Okay, now she had gone too far. Brayden was mine. Walking out from behind Hudson and Brayden, I got right in Sophie's face. Since she was sitting down, it brought us to about even so I could look her in the eye.

"Allow me to clear a few things up for you, Sophie. Do you see these highly attractive men behind me? I know you do, because you've been molesting them with your eyes since we met. They are off limits," I all but growled.

Sophie blinked at me, looked around me at the guys, and then brought her attention back to me. "And who are you to declare such a statement?"

"I'm their motherfucking girlfriend, and wife to that one," I announced, pointing at Brayden, whose eyes went wide with shock.

Parker was doing everything in his power not to burst out laughing, causing his face to turn bright red. Micah just shook head at me, but I could see the humor shining in his sapphire eyes. Jay, of course, didn't look any different, other than to have a hint of a smirk on his face. Hudson surprised me by taking my hand and threading our fingers together, bringing it up to his mouth and placing a kiss on the back of it.

Sophie gaped at me, speechless for the first time since we had met her. "*Non!* My, how very French of you, *mademoiselle*. I have to say, I am impressed that you can manage that amount of such men."

Taking a deep, calming breath, seeing that she was going to back off, I relaxed. "Thank you. Now, we do need to speak with Hudson's mother. Is there a time you can get us in? Also, we need some employee files. Can you gather them for us on a portable drive?"

"I would need to know what employees to pull, but I don't think that will be a problem."

Brayden stepped closer, putting his arm around my waist. "We need all the employees who worked on the nineteenth and twentieth and haven't been back since."

"*Tu es serieuse?* Do you know how many people that is? How exactly are you planning on going through all of them?" Sophie gasped.

"Well, our plan was that you could load them onto a portable drive or a tablet with access so we can work off-site and not disrupt things here," Brayden explained.

"For this you will need to speak with Mademoiselle Dupont. I cannot do this without her approval. Give me a moment to reach out to her personal assistant and see what I can do,"

Sophie said, picking up the phone and speaking rapid French to whoever was on the other line before she hung up again. "She will see you now."

CHAPTER 10

HUDSON

I'd never been in my mother's office before, and I wasn't surprised to see it was all white and completely modern looking. Her need to have perfect control over everything wouldn't allow her to have much self-expression in such a setting. This was the corner office of a powerful CEO, and the woman behind the desk lived up to that description.

"Why are you here, Hudson? I thought we discussed you not being in the office during business hours," Isabelle demanded.

I could feel Lailah tensing behind me at how Mother was addressing me, but I couldn't let her blow up at my mother like she did Sophie. Mother would tear her apart. It was a special gift that she had, finding your weakness and exploiting it. Typically, she reserved that skill for business transactions and her children, but I wouldn't put it past her to lash out at Lailah because she was mad at me.

"Mother, it would seem that there wasn't as much to do in the labs as we thought. What we need now is access to employee files," I stated, keeping to the facts.

Mother narrowed her eyes at me. "That still does not answer

the question of why you are in my office at this moment. Sophie should have been able to get you any information you needed."

Lailah, ignoring the way I tried to pull her back, shook off my hand. "Ms. Dupont, I am sorry we are intruding, but we did ask Sophie first for the things we needed, and she said you would have to give clearance for the number of files we need and permission to work on this off-site. We know you don't want us to disrupt things, so we thought working at the house would be best."

Mother slowly stood and walked around her desk, approaching Lailah. To Lailah's credit, she didn't back down—she never did when she was protecting one of us.

"I know who you are, Synergy. *Tu putes* is more like it, sleeping with all these boys like there is nothing wrong with it. If Hudson was truly my son, I would have never allowed him to attach himself to the likes of you," Mother sniffed, crossing her arms and looking down at her.

You didn't have to know French to know that my Mother just used some sort of derogatory term at Lailah. Watching Lailah carefully, I saw the hurt flash in her eyes before she covered it up, trying to keep a blank face. I had grown up most of my life dealing with this woman, used to her venomous tongue, but Lailah didn't deserve to be talked to like that at all.

"That is enough, Mother," I snapped, pulling Lailah behind me. "I do not care what your personal opinions are, but you will show some respect to her as someone I treasure. Now, will you give us the files we need so we can work at home, or do I need to bring this to the board's attention?"

Mother held my gaze, checking to see if I was bluffing or not, but I wasn't backing down from this. "*Stupide garçon*, you would let this woman ruin everything you have worked for? These Elementi are taking everything from you and your father. Don't you see it? Already you cannot live a normal life with the powers you have, now you let them tell you who to love?" Shaking her head, she waved us off. "Take what you need, but I don't want to see you back in this building during business hours, no matter who calls to try and overrule my authority. I'll have you arrested for trespassing."

"Have it your way, Ms. Dupont. We won't bother you any further," I said coldly.

All my life I'd been trying to gain her favor, but it was becoming clear to me now that she was never going to give it to me. I wasn't a son to her, for all she let me call her "Mother." That was going to change now. No longer was I going to cling to a childish fantasy when I could build a new family that wanted me around.

Lailah took my hand, intertwining our fingers as we walked out of the office without a backward glance.

Armed with the information we needed on a thumb drive and a few tablets, we headed back to the house. I wanted to distance myself from the lab and my parents after everything we had learned today. It was late afternoon once we exited the building.

"What if we went out for lunch? It might do us good to have a little break before we dive into these files," Lailah suggested.

"Yeah, I like that idea! This is supposed to be Christmas break, and we've hardly done anything fun," Parker whined.

Looking at the others, I raised a brow. "Everyone else okay with that?"

"If it means stalling looking at paperwork for however long, then hell yes, please. Let's go do anything," Micah agreed.

"Alright, I'll have the driver take us into town and we'll go find something that looks good to us," I said, turning to the driver and letting him know the change in destination.

Shortly after, we found ourselves walking through Old Town, where the buildings were packed together, forcing you to walk or bike through this part of the city. Shops spilled out of their stores onto the cobblestone alleys. Cafes with their doors open, tables scattered with people drinking and eating lined the street. This was the heart of the city that brought the magic to this place.

I couldn't keep the smile off my lips as I watched Lailah take it all in. Her love of architecture and history was showing full force. Parker joined in her fun, grabbing odd hats and other things off the vendors' tables and trying them on, making her laugh. Brayden grinned like a fool, no doubt being flooded with her emotions and energy, and even Micah and Jay seemed to be enjoying themselves. Eventually, we all decided to eat at a small cafe that had a good view of the beach and the sea.

"Guys, I have no idea what half this stuff is on the menu." Lailah sighed, looking at me for help. "Hudson, could you just order something for me?"

My heart warmed at the fact that she trusted me to make that choice for her, knowing she wouldn't understand me as I ordered. "I would be happy to. Anything you hate or are allergic to?"

"I don't care for olives or mushrooms, but I'm not allergic to anything," she answered with a grateful smile.

Parker elbowed me as he leaned closer. "Any chance you can help a bro out and tell me if they have pizza?"

"You want to order pizza in France?" Micah asked in disbelief. "Do you have any culture to you at all?"

Parker leaned back in his chair, crossing his arms. "What the fuck, man? Why'd you have to go and announce it to the whole table? I was trying to be discreet."

"That makes no sense. We would have seen what you ordered when you got it," Micah countered.

"So what are you getting, Micah?" Lailah asked, cutting into their argument.

"I'm going to get the catch of the day since we are here on

the coast. I never pass up fresh fish since we live so inland," Micah shared, giving Parker a smirk.

"Jay, what are you gonna choose?" Lailah inquired, turning to our ever-silent member.

"Ratatouille."

Parker rolled his eyes. "Of course you would pick the healthy option. You do know we are on vacation, right?"

"No, Parker, we are not on vacation. We are on a mission, an important one, which you would know if you took anything seriously," Jay corrected, stunning us all as he chided Parker.

"What the hell is going on with you guys today? Do I have a 'fuck with Parker' sign on my back I didn't notice?" he demanded.

"Usually," Micah muttered behind his hand.

I could see the tensions rising at the table now that we didn't have the distraction of the chaos around us. "Guys, we cannot have this discussion here. Let's wait until we get back to the house and we can hash it out then."

"Fine. If we can't talk about that, then how about we talk about your so-called mother and the shit she was saying to Lailah?" Micah snapped.

"Oh, and the fact she claimed us as boyfriends and Brayden as her husband. I think that deserves a few moments of our attention as well," Parker added.

All eyes turned to Lailah as he said that. Her cheeks were bright red, her blush setting her eyes off and making her more beautiful than she already was.

"I don't actually think we need to talk about that," Lailah said, fidgeting. "It was Parker's idea to claim you all, so I did. There's nothing more to talk about."

She was given a momentary reprieve when the waiter came over and took our orders, then dropped off our drinks. Unfortunately for her, Parker was not backing down from this and was like a dog with a bone.

"Sorry Trouble, but you are *so* not getting out of this. Now, tell me again what we are to you?" Parker grinned, pleased that Lailah was blushing beet red.

Taking a large gulp of her wine that I'd ordered her, she braced herself. "If I was wrong to call you all my boyfriends, I'm sorry, but I couldn't stand the way she was eying you all up. It's just rude to do that like you're a piece of meat or something."

"Especially when their girlfriend is standing right there to see it," Parker agreed, nodding his head.

"Exactly," Lailah exclaimed, then paused. "Wait—what did you say?"

"Oh, so you can call us your boyfriends, but we can't call you our girlfriend?" he goaded.

"I think 'wife' has a better ring to it, myself," Brayden chimed in, causing Lailah's eyes to widen in shock.

Lailah opened her mouth to say something a few times but just ended up closing it, unable to get the words out.

"You know, Lailah, we would have been calling you our girl-friend much sooner if you didn't want us to keep it a secret from everyone at school," Brayden pointed out. "You made that call, so don't be so shocked. I think we've all made it fairly obvious how we feel about you."

Hearing Brayden say that, it struck me that I was the only one who had not shown her how I feel. I'd told her that I am interested in her and that I know that we will end up being together—which is far from romantic. Even Jay made his inten-tions glaringly obvious with that stunt he pulled this morning. Thankfully, the only reason I heard it is because my room is directly under hers; it would have mortified her if either of my siblings had heard instead. Situations like these were why I was so on board with sharing her between us. In relationship and physical matters, I was ignorant. I've never slept with anyone before. The one time Parker got me drunk, some random woman gave me a blow job at a party, but I didn't want fake intimacy. It was the real thing or nothing for me.

"That was unfair of me, wasn't it," Lailah said dejectedly. "I was so worried about the backlash I didn't think of how you guys would take it. I'm sorry for that. Starting now, I don't want to hide our relationship. But I think calling me your wife might be a lot for people to take in when they figure out I have four other boyfriends."

Parker laughed, and the rest of us followed suit, thinking of people's reactions.

"Well, there's an easy way to fix that," Parker pointed out. "We gotta get a move on with this whole Bond thing."

Micah glared at Parker. "This isn't something you take lightly, fuckwit. It's better to not commit than to do it for the wrong reasons."

"It's gonna have to happen eventually! If we want to keep our girlfriend from having dream conversations with the Dark Lord, or her power fluctuating when the demon venom fucks with her, then I suggest we stop dicking around the subject," Parker retorted.

"Stop it," Lailah snapped, cutting in before Micah could say his piece. "Let us enjoy our dinner. No one is allowed to talk about anything having to do with demons... or school."

With a few grumbles, everyone agreed just in time for our food to arrive.

CHAPTER II
LAILAH

After we returned from lunch, we spent the rest of the day with tablets and computers going over the employee files. We took note of who had filed for time off and when that was submitted versus the people who just had normal days off or hadn't returned at all. It was monotonous and slow-going since we had to check in several different places to find everything we needed to rule someone out.

The following day was the same. We got up, ate, and went right back to work. Since it was Christmas Eve tomorrow, we wouldn't have much time since we were all going over to Mr. Lacy's place for the day. Something told me that would be the closest thing to a real Christmas, because I didn't see Ms. Dupont making merry.

Late in the day, I was sitting out on the second-floor veranda, enjoying the breeze and the scenery. The others were scattered throughout the house, not as content to be still the same way I was. With my headphones on while listening to music, I didn't notice anyone sitting next to me on the oversized chaise lounge until I was tapped on the shoulder.

Snapping my head to the right, I found Hudson's blue gaze alight with a smile.

"You scared me," I gasped, pulling my headphones out.

"Sorry. I called your name a few times, but you obviously didn't hear me."

"It's fine, clearly I was too invested in this project to pay attention to my surroundings." I smiled and bumped my shoulder against his. "What's up?"

Hudson seemed to pause, as if he was second-guessing himself in whatever he wanted to bring up.

"Hey, you can talk to me about anything," I reassured him.

"Do you really consider me your boyfriend?" Hudson asked, not looking me in the face.

Stunned by his question, I didn't answer right away. "Why do you ask?"

"I see how intimate you are with all the others, but not with me. Sure, you come to me when you need someone to help you figure things out logically, but that's something you could easily do with a friend as well."

Never had I expected this from Hudson—maybe Parker, but not Hudson. My fear of him being around his stepmother was coming true. Since the showdown in her office yesterday, the one I thought might help him to move forward, he had been set back more. Even though we didn't see Isabelle again after that, I could tell it was eating away at him.

Shifting, I set down the tablet and sat cross-legged next to him, giving him my full attention. "Hudson, do you truly believe that I don't care for you the same as I do the others?"

I needed him to admit how far his mother had gotten into his head.

"I don't want to believe it, Lailah, but I have doubts worming their way into my brain, and I can't seem to fight it," Hudson answered honestly.

Cupping his cheek in my hand, I lifted his face so I could look him in the eye. "Hudson Lacy, if you asked me to Bond with you right this minute, I would without question say yes. Brayden might keep me grounded when I get lost, but you, you are my trusted confidant. I know that I can come to you with anything that is weighing on me and we will figure it out together, no matter what it is."

I paused to see if anything I was saying was hitting home, but I still saw the shadow of doubt. "You brought up that I wasn't as intimate with you, but I never got a signal from you that it was important. After having someone use my emotions before, I would never want for anyone to give me what they weren't ready and willing to give. I think you're damn sexy and would climb you like a tree, as Cami would say, but I didn't think you wanted me to."

This seemed to surprise Hudson. "You didn't think I wanted you?"

"No, that is not what I said. Never did I have doubt you wanted me, but everything you do is with precision and timing. I was not going to push you when I knew you would get to it when you were ready."

Full understanding flashed in his eyes seconds before he grabbed my arms and pulled me forward, our lips crashing together. It was a desperate kiss, and yet at the same time tentative, still questioning if I was alright with it. I wrapped my arms around his shoulders and shifted so that I was straddling him, our chests pressed together.

With the torrent of emotions flowing around us, I could feel my powers reach out and caress his. I pulled back from him just enough that I could see his face.

"Just know that if you are not ready and say no right now, I will wait for you, no matter how long," I whispered.

"I'm done waiting, Sunshine," Hudson answered as he unleashed his powers.

There was a flash of light, and when it diminished, I was

standing, with Hudson kneeling before me. "Hudson Lacy, Knight blessed with Water's power, Warrior for the angels. I find you true of heart and mind, upholding the agreement given to your ancestors. Do you accept the eternal bond to protect the people of this world, and vow to cherish the vessel that holds the gift of Synergy, who has been placed in your protection?"

"I, Hudson Lacy, Blessed Elementi Warrior gifted with Water's power, vow to cherish and protect this world, my fellow brothers, and the one bound to us as Synergy; or my life be forfeit," Hudson answered, holding up his dual pistols to me.

"Rise, faithful one, and seal your Oath," I intoned as the angel's presence left me. Hudson scooped me up, wrapping my legs around his middle, and headed inside to my room.

I couldn't keep from kissing him as we fumbled our way down the hall, running into walls. His hands kneaded my ass as I clutched the back of his neck, unable to get close enough to him.

"We need to warn the others so we don't have Micah busting down the door again," I mumbled against his lips.

"No need. We just passed Parker in the living room; I'm sure he'll figure out what we're up to."

I couldn't help but laugh at that response as he kicked the door closed and tossed me down on the bed. He crawled up my body, placing kisses as he went even though I was still fully clothed. Once he reached my lips, he dove in, taking his sweet time exploring every inch. I groaned, as I wanted to feel more of him against me, but he still held his body above mine.

Frustrated, I let out a little growl before I pulled him down and flipped us over so I was on top. Grabbing the bottom of my shirt, I pulled it over my head and tossed it behind me, followed by my bra. Hudson watched the show with wide eyes, filled with hunger and amazement.

Then something struck me. "Is this your first time?"

Hudson licked his lips and nodded his head. "Yes."

"Am I going too fast?" I asked, worried that I was being too aggressive.

"No, I really like that you are taking charge and putting me at your mercy," Hudson said, letting his hands rove over my bare skin. "All I want to do is bring you pleasure and satisfy your needs."

Heat flared through my body at his words. "God, that has to be one of the sexiest things anyone has ever said to me."

"I am a blank slate, Sunshine. Teach me how I can please you."

Groaning, I dropped my head to his chest, unsure of what I wanted to happen first. "Clothes. Clothes have to go. I need to feel you against me, because right now I don't believe this is happening."

Without any more prompting, Hudson rolled me off of him and shucked off his shirt. Then he stood and removed his pants along with his underwear, baring himself fully to me. His body was toned but not overly so, and his golden skin shone in the setting sunlight, making my mouth water. Bending down, he unbuttoned my jeans and stripped them off of me so there were no more barriers between us.

He took his time taking me in, letting his gaze wash over me, making me blush. I sat up and took his hand, pulling him back to the bed to lay beside me. Tossing my leg over his hip, I held him closely to me, listening to his rapid heartbeat under my ear as I let my hands run down his back. He mimicked every touch I made as we explored each other.

"Sunshine, you are the most beautiful woman I have ever seen," Hudson said against my neck as he placed gentle kisses along my collarbone. "To think I get to spend the rest of my life with you, learning everything about this body of yours."

Gasping as he took my nipple into his mouth, I clutched at his hair. He had to be taking notes of my reaction with every nibble, lick, and bite, because he was driving me wild. After spending an equal amount of time with each breast, he moved lower and lower, watching me squirm as he stopped just above where I wanted him most.

"Just to put your mind at ease, my Sunshine, I might be new at this, but I have conducted extensive research," he said with a smirk before removing his glasses and setting them on the nightstand. "The key is to find what will apply best to you."

Before I had a chance to say anything, his mouth latched on to my bud and sent me arching and moaning with pleasure.

"If my assumptions are correct, that reaction was a positive one. Let's try something else, shall we?"

Hudson trailed a finger around my clit slowly, then applied pressure, dead center, causing me to pant and wriggle under him. Dipping his finger lower, he slid it inside me and bent it up like he was telling me to come, and come I did. With a shout of surprise, I sat up, clutching the comforter in my hands as he continued the movement, making my body spasm.

"Holy fucking shit!"

Hudson gave a low chuckle as I flopped back down to the bed. "Seems that move is a favorite."

"If anyone says that research is a waste of time, I will be the first to tell them to shut the hell up," I shared as I was still trying to catch my breath.

Hudson crawled up onto the bed next to me and scooped me up, pulling me on top of him. "For my first time, I want you to watch you, Sunshine, for you will be the only woman to ever ride me."

Catching him in a kiss, I nibbled on his lower lip as I slid myself onto him. We both moaned together as he filled me; it was a bit of a struggle, as he was thicker than Brayden. Relaxing into the fullness, I rocked slowly, watching the pure ecstasy that was written all over Hudson's face. It did something to my ego to know that I was the reason it was there, causing me to do more to see what other faces he would make.

Lifting myself up slightly, my hands on his pecs, I swirled my hips around, triggering a hissing sound to come out of Hudson. Pushing back, I sat up straight and rode him hard, his hands gripping my hips so tight I might have bruises to show after this. Heavy breathing and the sound of slapping skin was all you could hear, each of us lost in the sensations of our bodies.

Hudson started to buck more erratically under me, and I knew he was getting close. Leaning forward, lowering my body to his, needing more friction on my clit, I sped up, urging us both to the finish line. As we cried out, the walls rattled with our powers, and once again it lifted us up off the mattress as our souls were joined forever.

Toppling back down, we were a mess of limbs and naked skin glistening in sweat. I could feel Hudson's shock at our connection and the depth of his feelings that I never would have guessed being buried so deep.

"I can feel you, as if what you're feeling is an echo in my mind," Hudson said in awe.

Cradling his face in my hands, I kissed him on the forehead and then the lips. "There's no hiding from me now, Mr. Lacy."

"I wouldn't even try, my sweet Sunshine."

CHAPTER 12
LAILAH

After sneaking into the bathroom and sharing the shower since neither one of us wanted to be far from the other, we finally had to separate so we could get dressed and find the others, knowing that we all needed to talk after this happened. I only hoped that the power surge didn't affect the rest of the house and we didn't need to make something up for Hudson's siblings.

As I was headed out of the room, I caught what I was wearing in the mirror. It just so happened I grabbed my *I just want to cuddle, eat cookies, and drink chai tea* shirt. I thought about changing it but decided against it. Eventually I would be *cuddling* with all of these boys, and we all needed to get comfortable with it. Taking a deep breath, I made my way to the upstairs sitting room, where I guessed they would be waiting. This was not a conversation that anyone else should be overhearing.

"Did you two have fun?" Parker asked as he sat up from where he was sprawled out on the couch, patting the seat next to him. "Have a seat, I would love to hear all about it."

Ignoring Parker, I went over to Brayden in one of the armchairs and sat on his lap. He wrapped his arms around me and nuzzled his face against my neck. The other two were already here as well but were wise and didn't say anything. Moments later, Hudson came up the stairs, taking a seat on the furthest end of the couch from Parker. I could feel his embarrassment even though his face was carefully blank.

Oh, this was going to come in handy.

"If you guys are trying to find a way to not make this awkward, I don't think it's going to happen," Parker pointed out.

For once, Parker was right, but I wasn't going to say that out loud. Instead, I shifted so I could see Brayden better. "Did you notice anything change after we Bonded?"

"Yeah, nothing too exciting, but I can *feel* where Hudson is now. Like, if he left here and didn't tell us where he was going, I would know right where to find him. I can't feel his emotions like I can yours, but I know that he is fine and not in danger," Brayden explained.

"I have to say, that makes me feel better," Hudson interjected. "Having one person who can know everything about how I'm feeling is going to take some getting used to, but having all of you would have been overwhelming."

Brayden gave me a squeeze as he rested his head on my shoulder. "How are you feeling? Notice any differences now that you are Bonded to two of us?"

I paused for a moment and took stock of myself. The one thing I did notice was that in the space that my power resided, I could see a small ball of blue energy had joined the orbit around my power with the green one. Then again, I hadn't seen any change after I bonded with Brayden until I had to use my powers, so it might be the case this time as well.

"Nothing is sticking out to me, but as we have learned, that can always change," I answered, looking at all the others with a smile. "Is there anything else we need to talk about, or can we move on to other things?"

Parker raised his hand, making me smile as I nodded for him to ask his question.

"Can we revisit you sleeping alone? I mean, we all know Jay found his way into your bed at some point—not that I care," Parker said, holding up his hands to ward off the others, who were glaring at him. "I'm just curious is all."

"If you five can come up with some agreed-upon system, then I'm open to the idea," I answered with a smirk, knowing if I didn't they would all be trying to sneak into my bed.

Hudson cleared his voice, drawing everyone's attention. "How is everyone doing with the employee files?"

Jay grabbed his tablet from the side table and started to tap away at it. "I have ten possibilities with another fifty to go through. Since the Elementi have a base of operations here, we should send our findings to them and confirm the information."

"Wait, you want the Elementi to go door to door and check to see if they are really gone or that they are really the people they say they are?" Brayden asked.

"Both," Jay said, pausing to look up. "You can put anything down in your employee file; there is no way to tell if any of this information is correct or not. Feet on the ground is the best move, but it will be done more efficiently if a trained team does it."

"So what happens after we are done with this part?" I questioned.

Jay held my gaze as he answered. "We go back to Ryevick."

"What? Why?" I blurted. "That doesn't make any sense. Any clues we have are here."

"True, but we are not the right people to take this further. We will be needed elsewhere," Jay countered. "The serum is out there, and it's going to be used. When that happens, it'll be up to *us* to deal with it."

I wanted to argue with him, fight for us to stay here and see this through to the end, but I knew he was right. None of us had the training to take this further than we already had. We had discovered many things that other Elementi wouldn't see the same way we did, but now it was crossing over into the normal world, and none of us were prepared to deal with the legality of it all.

"Then I propose that we push and try and finish tonight so we can enjoy Christmas Eve without this lingering," I said, pushing myself off of Brayden's lap to find the tablet I'd been working on.

We all managed to finish the task and send off all the suspicious files to the Elementi here in France. It took us late into the night, but we wouldn't have to worry about it and could enjoy the last few days here in Nice. Heading off to my room, I changed into my pajamas and settled into bed. Grabbing my phone, I double checked the time back home and saw that it was six-thirty in the morning, so my mom would be up.

LAILAH:

Merry Christmas Eve! Hope you guys haven't been snowed in. We had a small change of plans and I'm in France, of all places. Hudson's parents live here in Nice.

MOM:

Merry Christmas Eve to you too, Ladybug! Oh, how exciting is that, you little world traveler you. Have fun with your friends and send me some pictures. I've always wanted to go to France.

LAILAH:

I will! Love you guys, miss you tons!!

MOM:

We love you too. Can't wait for summer when I can have you home. Then I can finally meet these friends of yours.

Since I'd moved into the Manor, my parents had video chatted with all the boys and Beth, wanting to make sure that me moving in was an appropriate option for me. Of course I couldn't tell her it was the *only* option just yet, but I was working on a way to figure out how to do that.

Just as I was going to turn my light off, Hudson walked in wearing just a pair of sleep pants. I tried to keep my emotions in check as I took him in, but the blush on his cheeks told me that I didn't do a very good job. Lord, it was like we were both little kids, embarrassed about seeing a little skin when only a few hours ago we were both completely naked.

"How did you manage to get first dibs on staying here tonight? Figured they would have objected since we already had *cuddle* time," I teased.

Hudson slid into bed and took off his glasses before rolling over to face me. "They put up a fight alright, but I had logic on my side."

"Are you going to tell me what that means?" I asked, having not a clue what he was talking about.

He reached out, grabbed what he could of my pajamas, and pulled me close to him. Snuggling in, I tucked my head under his chin and hitched a leg over his hip. The koala hold was my favorite way to sleep, I'd discovered.

"Well, you explained previously that you consider yourself married to Brayden after being Bonded. So if that is the case, then tonight would be our wedding night."

I couldn't help but laugh. "Oh, I'll bet they hated that argument."

"That may be, but I'm still here with you wrapped around me, so I see this as a win—don't you?"

"Well played, Mr Lacy. Well played," I murmured as Hudson kissed the top of my head and I drifted off to sleep.

The next morning found us all at the breakfast table, but this time everyone was chatting and the mood was much more relaxed. It was Christmas Eve, after all, and we would all be heading to Mr. Lacy's house. Ben and Grace were much more interactive and told us all about what the plan for the day was.

"The most important thing we have to do today is get the Christmas tree!" Grace told us as she clapped her hands.

"I wondered why you didn't have one up already," I mentioned.

Grace paused at this and gave Ben the side eye before she seemed to deflate a little. "Oh, well, Mother doesn't really like to have one in the house. She says it's too messy and we only have it up for a week or so anyway, so it's not worth it."

I was a little shocked at this, although I'm not sure why. Since Hudson's confrontation at the office, we hadn't run into his mother. I wasn't sure if she was avoiding us or if this is what they meant by her being gone a lot.

"When is your father expecting us?" Brayden asked, ever the one to need to be on time.

"If Grace has anything to say about it, the sooner the better," Hudson said, giving his sister a look that made her smile.

Just as Grace was going to add in her thoughts, Isabelle walked into the room. "Grace and Ben will not be going with you. They will be staying here."

I gasped as I felt rage rocket through me, and I knew it was coming from Hudson even as his face showed none of it.

"Why would that be?" he asked.

"They cannot afford to take the time away from their stud-ies," Isabelle offered, crossing her arms. "I may not be *your* mother, but I am theirs, and what I say goes."

"You're wrong. According to the court's ruling, Father is entitled to spend time with them on Christmas Eve. Just like he has to make sure they are back on Christmas day for you to be with them—or did you forget those details?" Hudson shot back.

Isabelle gaped at him in shock. Try as I might, I couldn't hold back my smile at her reaction, so I grabbed my coffee, trying to hide it.

"How could you possibly know that?" she asked, floundering with her response.

Hudson stood and put both his hands on the table as he looked the only mother he'd ever known in the face. "For this exact reason. There is absolutely no reason that Ben and Grace shouldn't come with us to spend time with *their* father. Do you not even see how hard both of your children try to please you? Of course not, because you would need to be around for that to happen. Ben could get into any school he wanted, even with the two Bs you seem to be lording over him. Grace is graduating a whole year early! Most parents would be thrilled to have two such accomplished children." Hudson paused to take a breath, closing his eyes a moment before he continued. "I made sure to read over the divorce agreement so you couldn't use them as a tool to get back at Father. We will be leaving now, *with* both of my siblings, and they will be back tomorrow. The rest of us will not."

Unable to provide an argument for anything Hudson said, Isabelle turned on her heel and stormed out of the room.

"That's it, I'm calling it. Bonding with Lailah definitely causes us to level up—because that shit was amazing, Hudson!" Parker announced, breaking the tension.

Grace was the next one to kick back her chair and run over to Hudson, throwing her arms around him. "I can't believe you stood up to her, thank you!"

"It seems like we should get packing before the wicked witch of the west kicks us out," Micah muttered as he got up from the table next to me.

Reaching down, he grabbed my hand, pulled me up, and tugged me after him as he headed upstairs. We walked into the room he was sharing with Brayden, and he directed me to sit on the bed he'd been using.

"Um, everything okay?" I asked, my brows raised.

Micah started to move about the room, gathering things. "Why does something need to be wrong? Maybe I just want to spend a little time alone with you." He paused and looked at me. "You okay with that?"

Just when I think I'm starting to figure these guys out, they pull shit like this.

"Totally okay with that. I'm sorry I didn't realize sooner that you were feeling this way," I answered, feeling guilty I hadn't realized it myself.

"None of that," Micah ordered as he walked over and cupped my chin, forcing me to look up at him. "It's just as much my responsibility to tell you I need some time with you. There is only one of you in this relationship of six. Hudson has needed you more the past few days, and we all know that."

"When did you get so insightful?" I asked, grinning.

Micah shook his head at me and dipped down to give me a forceful, all-consuming kiss. Pulling back slightly, he winked at me. "Looks like you might need to hang around me more to notice."

"Micah, are you flirting with me right now?" I teased.

His answer was to push me down onto the bed, using his body to pin me down but not smother me. Sliding his hands in my hair, he held me where he wanted me as he proceeded to show me just how much he missed me. Reaching up, I pulled out his hair tie, letting his thick, wavy locks free for me to return the favor.

"Pardon the interruption, I'm just going to start packing my things while you two are busy," Brayden said from somewhere in the room.

Micah pulled back and shifted to the side so he could pull me into being the little spoon. "What, you don't want to join in?"

Brayden looked over at the two of us, cocking an eyebrow and setting his hands on his hips. "Oh, I didn't think we were at that level yet. Have you finally decided to take the Oath and Bond with her?"

I snorted as I tried to hold in my laughter but utterly failed once Micah started poking me in the side.

"Think that's funny there, Cookie Monster? I'll give you something to laugh about," Micah grumbled as he proceeded to tickle me until I was gasping for breath.

"Bryaden, help me," I cried.

"Sorry, Angel, you got yourself into that one," Brayden sighed as he packed his things like nothing was going on.

"Do you surrender?" Micah demanded as he kept on with his attacks.

"I give up, you win," I gasped.

Micah stopped but loomed over me, his nose touching mine. "Bet your ass I win. Now, go pack your shit. Can't have you holding up the rest of us."

I huffed indignantly at him. "Oh right, because that would be *my* fault how?"

"Don't sass me, woman. Get going," Micah ordered, giving my ass a slap, sending me towards the direction of the door.

"Oh, you did not just do that!" I gasped.

Micah smirked at me. "Sure did. Now move along or I'll do it again."

Frowning, I walked out into the hall, crashing into Jay. Quickly, his hands settled on my hips as I bounced off him, a soft smile on his lips. "Spanking is on the table now? That is going to make things much more fun."

"I never agreed to that."

Jay leaned down and nipped at my ear. "Oh, I have a feeling you will, Beautiful."

CHAPTER 13

LAILAH

M r. Lacy sent two cars to get all of us and our luggage since there was no way we would all fit in one with Ben and Grace joining us. Isabelle didn't show her face as we all left, which I was thankful for. No need to make things worse. The driver took us back into Old Town where Mr. Lacy's apartment was, which made me even more excited. The streets were filled with pop-up markets for presents and Christmas trees. Overnight, this place had turned festive. It wasn't as gaudy as I was used to back in the States; they used more natural decorations and ribbons versus glitter and lights.

Reaching our destination, the drivers helped us carry our things up the five flights of stairs to the top floor. A set of dark stained wooden French doors greeted us. Grace promptly pulled out her key and unlocked the door, flinging them both open as she bounced into the place.

"*Père*, we're here," Grace called out.

The difference between this place and Isabelle's couldn't have been more extreme. Here the furniture was overstuffed, covered in dark leather, and very welcoming. It had a rich, warm feeling to it that just made you want to light a fire and read a book. Just another sign to show how different the two of them were.

Mr. Lacy walked out from a room dressed in pressed slacks and an emerald-green sweater, looking far more relaxed than I had seen him.

"I feel so honored to have you all here for Christmas Eve, a wonderful surprise indeed," Mr. Lacy said with the biggest smile on his face.

Grace ran up to him, threw her arms around his waist, and hugged him tight. Mr. Lacy returned the hug and kissed the top of her head. "Well, my Gracy-goose, are you ready to show these guys how we do Christmas Eve?"

Pulling back just enough so she could look up at him, she nodded furiously. "Yup, but Hudson gets a special prize because *Mère* wasn't going to let us come. If he hadn't stood up to her, then we wouldn't have been able to have a Christmas here at all."

Chadwick's eyes narrowed, and his smile dimmed a little as he looked at Hudson. "I'm sorry you had to do that, son. You should have called me. I would have handled it."

"It was something I needed to do. It was time to stand up to her, to protect my family and do what's right, even if it's hard," Hudson said as he took my hand.

The pride I felt for Hudson was overflowing, and I made sure that he could feel it too. What he had done might not seem big to others, but it was another step in the direction of not hiding his feelings anymore.

Chadwick watched Hudson for a moment before he nodded his head. "I can understand that. Well done, son." Letting go of Grace, he clapped his hands before rubbing them together. "It's time to find ourselves a Christmas tree."

Already being in the heart of Old Town, all we had to do was walk out the front door of the building to find what we were looking for. Hudson took my left hand while Parker took my right, making me smile. As we wandered, inspecting tree after tree, I couldn't help having this feeling that this was the first time that I had ever felt completely content.

It was clear to see that this tree was important by the way Ben and Grace argued over each selection. Just when I didn't think we would find one, Ben gave a shout, causing Grace to race over to where he was. This tree was about six feet tall, and it was so full you couldn't even see the trunk through the branches. I don't think I'd seen a more picture-perfect tree in all my life.

"*Que c'est beau.* It's perfect," Grace said, smiling and clapping her hands.

Chadwick looked at the tree, then at us. "This is the moment that I always wished I'd had more help to bring home whatever they pick out. It seems to get bigger and bigger each year."

The guys laughed along with him, and the vendor tied up the tree so that it was easier to carry. It took four of them to lug the tree back to the apartment, but the real adventure was getting it up all the flights of stairs with the narrow twists and turns. Once back home, Grace grabbed my hand, and we raced off deep into the back of the apartment to a large closet.

"We keep all the decorations and everything else for Christmas here," Grace explained as she handed me boxes.

Unable to carry more, I headed off to the living room, where I assumed the tree would be set up. Placing the boxes down, I watched as Chadwick directed and Hudson and Ben tried to get the tree to stand up straight while Micah and Parker were tightening the stand underneath. I covered my mouth with my hands, trying to keep in the laughter.

"He said to stop tightening on your side, dipshit," Micah snapped as the tree tilted to the left.

Parker's head popped out front under the tree. "No, he didn't. If you actually listened to someone for once, Mr. Know-It-All, you would have heard him say it was you who needed to stop."

"Boys, if we could stay on the task at hand," Chadwick interjected unsuccessfully.

"Oh you wanna go, asshat?" Micah growled, rolling out from under the tree. "You wanna say that to my face this time?"

Just as I was about to step in, Jay walked up and grabbed them both by their ears and tossed them onto opposite sides of the large sectional couch. Both of them looked shocked at the action, eyes wide, Parker's jaw hanging open.

"We are guests in this house—act like it," Jay stated.

Without even raising his voice, Jay had managed to make both of them look chagrined and mumble out an apology. Satisfied, Jay dropped down to the floor and within moments had the tree secure and standing straight.

"What magic have you performed on our silent ninja?" Brayden asked into my ear as he wrapped his arms around my waist.

I jumped slightly but relaxed into his hold. "I don't know what you mean."

"There was a time not so long ago that Jay would have just walked away and left them to fight amongst themselves. He kept himself detached from all of us, knowing that his father disapproved. Ever so slowly, he is proving again and again that he will fight for us to be a team—hence why he wouldn't let them fight like that," Brayden said with his head resting on my shoulder. "You, my Angel, are the miracle we needed to make this whole thing work."

I let Brayden's love for me and the other people around us flow through me. Never in my life did I think I would have a boyfriend like Brayden, let alone someone who, for lack of a better word, was my husband. Wait—I had two husbands now that Hudson and I had Bonded.

"About time you guys finished with that, we have some serious decorating to do here. Ben, will you grab pens for everyone to write with?" Grace directed as she brought in more boxes. "I always make sure that we make some of our decorations each year; it means more that way. Anyone can put things on a tree and make it look nice, but that takes away from the spirit of Christmas, *non*?"

The more I got to see Grace away from her mother, the more I liked her. She reminded me of a milder version of Cami, in some ways, with her drive to make things fun. Ben, on the other hand, was just as quiet, but he didn't hunch his shoulders like he was waiting for the other shoe to drop, like he did at his mom's. Coming back with pens, he handed one to all of us and then Grace followed, passing out strips of green and red paper.

"Now, we are going to write our wishes for the new year on these. I'm giving everyone three, so if you have more wishes you can put them down. I know that personally I'm going to want more than one," Grace explained as she sat on the floor, legs crossed.

I had to agree that there was a lot that had changed in this year alone, and I didn't know what would happen in the next. Part of me was worried to even try and think about it, but I'd promised myself that I wasn't going to let the Dark Lord take away more from me than he already had. Walking over to the couch, I snuggled into the corner and grabbed a pillow to write on. I hunched over my work, not letting any of them see what I was writing. A girl had to keep some secrets. Just as I finished, I felt someone lean over the back of the couch, casting a shadow on my slips of paper.

"What are you wishing for, Trouble?" Parker asked from right beside my ear.

Quickly, I flipped the slips over so he couldn't see. "Nope, I'm betting the same rules apply to all wishes. You don't tell anyone what it is that you're wishing for or it doesn't come true."

"That's no fun," he whined, trying to give me puppy dog eyes. "How are we supposed to make sure your dreams come true if we don't know them?"

"Nice try, but I'm not going to tell you. Back me up here, Grace," I said, looking up to find her grinning at us both.

"I have to agree with Lailah. You can't tell people what you wish for." Grace smirked.

Leaning back into the couch, I looked up at him. "Nice try, but not quite good enough."

As Parker pouted at me, I gave him a peck on the lips but scooted out of the way when he tried to come back for more. I was not going to make out with one of my boyfriends in front of another's parent and siblings.

"Now what do we do?" I asked even though I had a guess.

Grace stood up and took the slips from me and everyone else. "I'll staple them together. That way no one will be able to peek."

"Lailah, would you help me in the kitchen while Grace directs the boys on the decoration process?" Chadwick asked with a soft smile.

"Of course, I would be happy to," I said, following him.

The kitchen was just off the living room with a door that led right into the formal dining room. It was far more simple than the one I'd glimpsed at Isabelle's, and there was no hired help to do the cooking, it seemed. Chadwick pulled down a large wooden board, setting it on the counter, then started taking things out of the fridge.

"If you wouldn't mind arranging all these things on the board while I cut up the cheese, that would be helpful," he asked, nodding to the array of items.

We worked in silence as I tried to organize foods I didn't recognize while he chopped cheese and some meat as well.

"Do you mind if I ask you a question?" Chadwick ventured.

I paused, scooping out the mini pickles to look up at him. The concern written all over his face made it hard to deny him what I knew he wanted to ask. "I don't mind, as long as you are alright if I don't answer it."

"That's fair," Chadwick agreed, resuming his task. "I know

that Hudson sees Isabelle as the closest thing he has to a mother, but I know she doesn't view him as a son. It was one of the major reasons we got divorced. At first, we tried to work it out for Ben and Grace since they were still at home with us, but I could tell it wasn't healthy." Chadwick seemed to pause and switch gears on what he was going to say. "Did you know that this is the first time in ten years that Hudson has been home for Christmas? When he was at boarding school he never came home, even on breaks."

Shocked, I snapped my gaze up to meet his. "Ten years? He told me it had been a while, but I just figured it was since he'd been at school."

"He was sent to the Elementi schools as soon as his powers presented. Isabelle didn't think it was safe to have him around Ben and Grace. I should have fought harder against her request, but I didn't know the first thing about dealing with any of that. I've always been a scientist, and it was my cousin that held the water element before Hudson, and I never interacted with him. In trying to do what was best for my son, I also sent him away and made him feel unwanted. We have always stayed in contact, and he kept saying that he would visit since I moved out, but he never did until now." Setting down his knife, he turned to me and grasped my hands. "I have seen the change that has come over him, and I know it's because of you. Thank you, Lailah. Thank you for giving me another chance with my son."

He leaned forward and placed a kiss on my cheek, making me blush at his heartfelt words.

"Um..." I started and cleared my throat. "You said you wanted to ask me something?"

"Right," he said, combing a hand through his salt-and-pepper hair. "Are Grace and Ben safe with their mother? I don't want what happened to Hudson to happen with them."

I thought about that question for a moment and wondered if answering it was even my place. Yes, I was now part of this family for better or worse, but they didn't know me and I didn't know them—not really. "I won't give you an answer to that question, but I do have a suggestion to help prevent something like that from happening, if you care to hear it."

"By all means." Chadwick gestured for me to continue.

"Find out what those two *really* want to do. Where do they want to go to college? What job truly interests them? Not what would be best for the family image, but what gets them excited about learning? They are extremely smart, kind, and they might even have talents that you don't even know about that they would like to pursue. I think if you let them know they are heard and their opinion matters, it will change everything," I answered with a shrug of my shoulders. "What could it hurt?"

"Indeed, what could it hurt..."

CHAPTER 14

LAILAH

The rest of the day was filled with fun, laughter, and quality time with each other. This is what it was like for me and my family during the holidays, and I didn't realize how much I had missed this in my life. After the tree was decorated, we played games until it was time to start making dinner. Chadwick had us all working in the kitchen, giving us our own assignments. Once he figured out that I was no stranger to cooking, he had me working on a few of the more involved dishes. It was enjoyable to learn a new style of food and the tricks they used for ingredients I hadn't worked with very often. Finally, it was time to sit down and eat.

"*Père*, we never use the formal dining room," Grace commented with a slight frown.

"Well, Goose, we never have this many people, and with the meal we made, it might be harder to manage sitting in the living room," Chadwick said, setting down the last serving dish.

Grace nodded her head and took a seat next to me, cutting off Parker at the same time.

"Ah, I was going to sit there, Grace," Parker complained.

"You get to be with her all the time. I, on the other hand,

have no idea when she will come back to visit," Grace stated as she placed her napkin in her lap.

Parker opened his mouth like he was going to argue, looking between me and the fifteen-year-old who had just outsmarted him. Letting out a heavy sigh, he moved on and took the seat next to Jay.

Grace turned to me with a slight frown. "How do you manage having so many boyfriends? I would think trying to deal with five needy men is a lot of work."

I couldn't help it. I burst out laughing at her sincere tone, like she genuinely wanted to know the answer. "I'm still figuring that out myself, Grace, since this is new for me still. Some days I'm better at it than others. Although, I was reminded the other day that it's not just on my shoulders to keep up with what everyone needs. We all have to communicate and share when a little extra attention might be needed. Otherwise, we do end up spending a large amount of time together as a group."

"Personally, I think I'm going to stick to only one boyfriend," Grace said with a nod of her head as she grabbed the platter of food in front of her.

The rest of dinner was pleasant, and once it was finished, we all helped out once again, cleaning up. Ben asked if we could watch a Christmas movie, and everyone thought it was a great idea. Snuggled up between Brayden and Micah with a blanket, I couldn't help but drift off to the sounds of *Santa Claus is Coming to Town*, Ben's movie of choice.

"Well, look at this. Little Synergy has Bonded with another one of her Knights. I hate to tell you this, but you're going to have to work a lot faster on that if you want to save yourself," the Dark Lord purred in my ear.

I was back in the void where he liked to taunt me, making me feel abandoned and alone.

I was getting sick of it.

"I know what you're doing with the serum, the new perfect hosts it creates for your demons," I shot back.

The Dark Lord chuckled, sending shivers down my spine. "You only know what I want you to know, child. Just because you've learned this tidbit doesn't mean you have a clue as to what I have planned for all of humanity."

"Why do you keep pulling me here to talk to me? Every time I give you the same answer, and then you threaten me. What's stopping you from just removing me from the equation?"

I felt the tip of a claw run along my jaw, causing me to hiss as it cut into my skin. "That was very short-sighted of me, wasn't it? I do have a problem with controlling my temper. You, my Little Synergy, just seem to bring out the worst in me. I'm not used to people telling me no."

"That didn't answer my question."

"Oh, but didn't it?"

"My answer is never going to change, no matter what you do," I growled as my frustration grew.

"Tut, tut now. I wouldn't be making such bold statements; they always have the habit of making me want you to *prove* it. You say that *nothing* could *ever* change your mind. What about these men you hold so dear? No, that's too direct—their families? Oh, I know! Your family," the Dark Lord taunted. "Would you really let them be taken and used, left to rot? You see, for them, I wouldn't use the serum. No, I would want you to watch them decay right before your very eyes. Doesn't that sound like fun?"

Fury like nothing I have ever known burst forth, my powers reacting to my anger. The darkness was suddenly filled with golden light, creating a protective bubble around me. Tendrils of darkness tried to pierce the barrier, but they sizzled against the light, drawing back.

"I will not let you lay a finger on any of the people I love! One day soon we will find you, and we WILL stop you. I'd stake my life on it," I screamed, hands fisted at my sides, shaking in anger.

Looming in the darkness, I could now see the Dark Lord's face, his eyes pools of darkness, teeth razor sharp. He let one claw-tipped hand scrape down along my barrier, testing it. I knew he could break through it if he wanted to, since I wasn't at my full potential with only two Knights bonded to me.

The Dark Lord tipped back his head and laughed, the sound shaking the ground I was standing on. "You ask why I don't kill you? Because if I can turn you, oh, how you would be the perfect weapon to have at my side. Never have I seen someone so pure who also harbors the blackest evil in their heart."

I wanted to argue, to tell him he was wrong, but with a flick of his wrist, I was thrown out of the darkness and back into reality.

"Someone better tell me what the hell is going on!" Chadwick bellowed.

Opening my eyes, I saw that I was now surrounded by a shield I had made in the darkness, Brayden clutching me to him.

"Lailah, you need to wake up. Please, Angel. I need you to come back to us. You are safe. We have you," Brayden murmured over and over in my ear.

"The Dark Lord must have pulled her into another conversation. It's the only time it happens these days," Hudson explained to his father.

"That doesn't make sense. This place is warded against any demon activity. He shouldn't have been able to get to her," Chadwick argued.

Shifting, I slowly sat up, pulling out of Brayden's arms, and the barrier dissipated as I took a few deep breaths. Everyone in the room had eyes only for me. Ben and Grace were standing huddled by the entrance to the kitchen, fear written on their faces. Hudson was standing next to his father, a hand on his chest as if he was holding him back from coming to me. Micah was sprawled out on the floor with his hair sticking out like he'd been electrocuted, and his clothes even seemed a little singed. Glancing around the room, I found that the shield had left burn marks in the couch and floor where it had been.

"What happened?" I gasped.

"We would all like to know the answer to that question, Lailah." Chadwick's voice was hard.

I tried to understand that he was scared and that what happened could have hurt someone, but I couldn't help but feel hurt by the anger and distrust in his eyes.

"Father, as I tried to explain before, the wards you have set up keep demons from entering, but that's not what the Dark Lord does to her. Lailah survived an attack from a Greater Demon, and even though she was cleansed, it didn't remove all the venom from her system. It seems that she can be pulled into some sort of limbo where the Dark Lord talks to her. We have tried many things to keep it from happening, but until we all Bond, we aren't strong enough," Hudson explained.

Chadwick looked at me, eyes narrowed. "Are you telling me this is a common thing that happens?"

I shook my head vigorously. "No, the Dark Lord has only started talking to me in the last week. I think he knew Hudson and I bonded and was upset about it, because this time he was much more aggressive in taunting me."

"I see," Chadwick said, relaxing slightly. "In light of this information, I am going to take Ben and Grace back to their mother's. I don't think it is a good idea for them to be around this. They have not been brought up knowing about the

Elementi. Although I have a feeling that will change after this incident."

My stomach dropped, and guilt started to squeeze my heart at his words. He was right. I was dangerous to people around me who didn't know the hidden darkness in our world.

"No, please wait. We will go," I said, standing.

Hudson and the others looked like they wanted to argue with me. "This is Christmas Eve, and you need to spend it with your children. Hudson will stay here, and the rest of us will find a hotel to spend the night in. I'm sure Ben and Grace will have lots of questions, and Hudson knows everything that's going on. He will be able to help you. None of us have unpacked, and it's safer to be just us while I'm clearly unable to control what happens with my powers."

None of my guys seemed happy with my decision, but I wasn't going to be moved on this. This was the world that we of the Elementi lived in, with our eyes wide open to the dangers. Hudson's siblings did not, and it wasn't fair to them—so we would leave.

"Thank you, Mr. Lacy, for an amazing day. I am so utterly sorry that I have caused a disruption to it." With that I bowed my head, gathered my things, and walked out the door, lugging my suitcase with me.

Moments later, my luggage was taken from me, and I looked up to find Jay. Looking into his wise, gray eyes, I knew he understood what I'd done and that he was supporting my choice. I could only imagine with the missions and other things he has done working for his father, this was a simple call. To me, though, it just showed me that no matter how much I wanted to pretend, I couldn't live a normal life with these simple, happy moments. Not until the Dark Lord was defeated.

I didn't need to look behind me to know that the rest of them had followed me, and from the sadness in my heart, I knew Hudson had stayed liked I asked. He had just gotten the chance to have his family back, and I damn well wouldn't be the reason he lost it again.

With a little bit of research, we found a hotel we could stay at. We got connecting rooms since they didn't have a room large enough to fit us all. They decided to leave the door open between us, but they all ended up in the room I was staying in. Jay sat in the armchair by the bed, Parker was laid out with my feet on his chest, and Micah and Brayden were on either side of me, leaning against the headboard. The TV was on, but the sound wasn't turned up since no one was really watching it.

Micah took my hand and lifted it to his lips, pulling my gaze to him. "You okay there, Cookie Monster? I'm sure that was a hard choice to make."

I closed my eyes and let the tears I'd been holding back trail down my cheeks. "He's right. Until this is over, I shouldn't be around people who aren't prepared to deal with the mess we bring."

"Trouble, I hate that you think that. Was this a shitty situation—yes. Doesn't mean it's your fault," Parker said, giving my feet a squeeze.

"Do you mind telling us what the Dark Lord wanted this time?" Brayden asked.

I really didn't want to tell them what happened because I knew how they would take it. The fact they can't protect me while I'm trapped in that dark world with him ate at them. Why should I add fuel to that fire?

"It was nothing new, he just wanted me to know he knew I'd added Hudson into the mix and that it still wouldn't be enough. The upside is that because I'm stronger, I was able to put up that shield... not that it helped much, but it didn't leave me in the dark," I shared, shrugging my shoulders.

I could feel the doubt coming from Brayden. He knew I was holding something back by the way I was acting. This is when having someone so tuned into your emotions was more of a hindrance.

"Lailah, you know you can tell us anything, right?" Brayden pushed, giving me the chance to come clean.

Resting my head on his shoulder, I nodded. "I do, but sometimes saying more is not always going to be helpful. He wants to show me just how much power he has, and every time I tell him no, it drives him crazy. The Dark Lord is used to getting his way, but I'm the wild card that gets to choose what side I want to fight for. Every time, he tries to pick away at things, trying to see what he can use against me. Unfortunately, this time he hit on something, and it made me lose my temper and show him he had something to work with. So he proceeded to taunt further until he found the perfect place to sink his claws into."

"What was it?" Jay asked.

I took a deep breath, not wanting to admit it, but I had to. They needed protection. "My family and you guys."

"I hate to say this, but I'm surprised he didn't go for that sooner. If he pays attention to you at all, he should know that the people you hold close to your heart are your weakness as much as your strength," Jay pointed out.

"True. If he hadn't made me that mad, I wouldn't have created the shield. I did it once before when the avalanche was happening, but I'd never tried it in that dream world. Nice to know that some tricks can be used in both places," I mused.

The room fell silent again, as we were all lost deep in thought.

"What do we do now?" Parker finally asked, unable to take the quiet any longer.

"Go back to Ryevick. I need to get working on my training, and it's safer there for whatever is going to happen with the serum. The one thing I don't doubt the Dark Lord on is following through on his threats." I sighed. "Something is going to happen, and we aren't going to like it."

CHAPTER 15

JAY

Finally, Lailah fell asleep, and the rest of us went into the other room, shutting the connecting door so we could talk. I could see the tension that everyone was carrying after she had told us about her most recent interaction with the Dark Lord. It seemed that I was the only one who wasn't surprised at this turn of events. Demons never play fair and always go for the soft spot we all have in our lives.

If you had asked me four months ago what my weakness was, I would have said my mother. My father, the bastard that he is, couldn't give two shits about her, abandoning her to live in Japan with her family. In his eyes, he had fulfilled his duty as man of the house by producing a male heir, and one that turned out to be an Elementi Warrior, at that. Try as he might to keep me under his thumb, I did things the way I wanted, even though on the outside it must look like I catered to him. It was situations like this with the Dark Army, where he kept holding things back from the Elementi organization that got people hurt or killed, that made me buck under his control even more. Especially now that I had a new weakness.

"What the fuck are we going to do? Should we have all our

families on high alert?" Parker asked, running his hands through his hair. "We have to tell Beth. God knows if we don't, she will just suffer in silence. Could you imagine if the Dark Lord or his people got to one of our family members—it would kill her."

Even though I understood where Parker was coming from, his reaction was completely blown out of proportion. Hudson's siblings were the only ones that didn't grow up knowing about the Elementi. Since I was an only child and so was Micah, it brought the pool of people down considerably. Brayden and Parker had the largest families, but after the events with Ms. Tabitha, I can only imagine that they would have already stepped up security. Not to mention the Elementi would put out a bulletin alerting everyone to what we found out about the serum and what dangers it poses to us.

"Lailah is who he is after, so I think it would be best to get some kind of protection for her family. There was a team watching her for weeks before she came to Ryevick, so it shouldn't be too hard to put them back in place," Brayden reasoned.

"Any chance I could offer up my aunt as a sacrifice?" Micah mused, tapping his chin.

I couldn't hold back a smirk at that thought.

"It's more likely that she's already possessed—that witch was awful," Parker said with a shiver.

Micah let out a bark of laughter. "Now I know the world is ending—I agreed with Parker again about something."

"Try not to make a habit out of it, will you? It's starting to freak me out." Parker frowned.

"Bringing us back to the matter at hand, we should get hidden protection for Lailah's family. Then the second piece to this needs to be her training. We have put it off for far too long," I interjected. "She is smart and picks things up quickly, but we need to fast track her on demons, self-defense, and figuring out what her powers can do. Everything else needs to be put on pause until we know she can protect herself if one of us isn't there."

"It's times like these that I can't understand why they don't think you're the smart one, Jay," Parker said with amusement bright in his eyes.

Since the day we all met, Parker had been trying to figure out what makes me tick. He still had yet to figure it out—not from lack of trying, though.

"No, he's right," Brayden agreed. "Lailah needs a more in-depth course on demons, and understanding how her powers work will also help us. I'm sure there are things I can do differently now that we are Bonded, but I haven't really had the chance to work with her on it. The same goes for Hudson. Who knows, there might even be a cool trick he and I can do. Now that we are both Bonded, I feel a new connection to him—nothing like what I have with Lailah, but still, it's worth figuring out."

"Then it's settled. Once Hudson is back, we will fly to Ryevick and start working on understanding our new dynamic," Micah said, getting to his feet and heading back to Lailah.

The three of us paused and looked at each other.

"Whose night was it supposed to be?" Brayden asked.

Parker raised his hand. "That would be me."

Brayden let out a heavy sigh and headed in to tell Micah the bad news. A few minutes and a lot of angry whispers later, they both returned. Micah stormed up to Parker and got right up in his face. "You better not lay a finger on her tonight. She needs to sleep. Meetings with the Dark Lord always wear her out, and with the amount of power she's expended and the emotional drama she's been through, she needs *rest*."

Parker frowned, eyes flashing with anger. "Why the fuck would you think I would take advantage of her?"

"Because you have this compulsion to get your way and pout

if you don't. She can't take a guilt trip right now," Micah snapped back.

Parker's power swirled around him in his anger. The happy-go-lucky man was gone, and a storm cloud of anger stood in its place.

"Lailah means everything to me! I would never do anything to hurt her emotionally or physically—unlike someone else. Since I met her that first week of school, all I've ever wanted was to be there for her, whether it was as a friend or something more. Nothing I have done has been to manipulate Lailah in any way, so take your judgment and shove it up your ass," Parker growled, shoving Micah away from him. "Maybe you should look in the mirror when you say shit like that, because I know damn well if she presents the chance for me to give my Oath, I'll be man enough to do it."

The room fell silent as Parker left, closing the door behind him firmly, showing restraint when he would normally have slammed it shut. None of us moved, too shocked at Parker's outburst to know how to react.

"What the actual fuck just happened? We all know what a player he is and Lailah isn't like all the other girls he sweet talked into sleeping with him. She needs it to mean something... hell everything," Micah spluttered as he pulled his hair out of its binding so he could comb his fingers through it.

Crossing my arms, I replayed what just went down. "It seems that we have stumbled onto the one thing that will set him off like a bomb."

"I didn't think that was possible," Brayden said, shaking his head. "Do we think it's safe to leave him with her while he's like that?"

"At this moment, I think Lailah is the safest woman in the world with him standing guard, but if we think it's a good idea, I can stay there with them," I offered.

They both nodded, looking more relaxed at the thought of

me being in there as well. It didn't cross my mind that Parker would do anything to Lailah, but tensions between Micah and Parker have always been high, and Brayden would always back Micah up. When I entered the room, I found Parker glaring at me from over Lailah's shoulder like a wolf protecting its prize.

"Why are you here? Did they send you to make sure I didn't molest her in her sleep?" Parker asked in a harsh whisper.

Lailah's face scrunched up, and she shifted, turning into Parker as if to soothe him.

"No."

That was the only answer I was going to give him as I lifted the covers and slid in beside Lailah. Laying on my back, I closed my eyes and refused to give into the argument that Parker wanted to have with me. I had every right, as one of Lailah's boyfriends, to sleep beside her, and I wasn't going to let him make me feel bad about it in the slightest.

CHAPTER 16

LAILAH

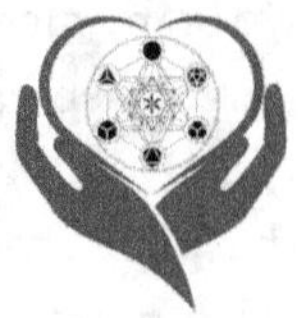

The next morning, I woke up sandwiched between Parker and Jay, an odd but welcome combination. What I found even more strange, though, was how my lighthearted prankster was brooding and silent. A tension hung in the air with the other guys, making my skin prickle with agitation. They all tried to act like nothing was wrong and kept things light as we headed down to eat breakfast, but I knew better.

By the time we had finished, Hudson arrived with the car that was going to take us to the airport. Even without the ability to feel Hudson's emotions, I could tell that last night had not gone well. He had bags under his eyes, and his shoulders slumped like he was too tired to fight against the world. The need to comfort and fix what was going on among my men made me fidget.

"Beautiful, if you don't stop squirming on my lap, we are going to end up with a situation that you are not prepared to fix at the moment," Jay whispered, his lips brushing along the shell of my ear.

Blushing, I forced myself to sit still. The car didn't have

enough room for all of us, so I was seated on Jay with his strong, muscular arms wrapped around my waist. Parker sat in the front seat, unwilling to be near the rest of the group, and would only speak if I talked to him directly.

So much for a merry Christmas. Seemed I needed to figure out what was going on with two of my men.

Boarding the plane, everyone spread out, but Hudson stuck close to my side, his hand firmly holding mine. The moment we were up in the air and the pilot announced that we were at cruising altitude, I unbuckled myself and pulled Hudson with me. I didn't even look at the other men, knowing I could only fix things one at a time.

Closing the door to the bedroom, hands on my hips, I looked at Hudson sitting on the bed. "What do you need from me?"

Hudson hung his head and shook it slowly, like he didn't even know what to ask for. Remembering how he craved my direction when we Bonded, I decided to try something I've never done before.

I placed my hand on his jaw and made him look at me, his blue eyes raw and lost in emotion that he never showed. "Scooch back on the bed and lay down on your side."

He looked like he wanted to argue with me, but I raised an eyebrow at him with a slight frown. Sighing, he kicked off his shoes and did as I asked, looking over at me as if to make sure he was doing it right. I crawled up beside him and gently removed his glasses before I made him the little spoon in our cuddling. Knowing how much I loved it, I combed my fingers through his hair and watched his eyes flutter closed.

"Rest. Don't think, don't overanalyze. Just listen to the sound of my heartbeat and keep your eyes closed," I murmured to him.

Within moments, his breathing evened and he fell asleep clutching one of my arms to his chest as I continued to play with his hair. Talking could happen later. At this moment, he just needed rest and to know he was safe and loved. When I was sure that he was soundly sleeping, I gingerly pulled away from him to deal with the other matters in the main cabin. As I walked back out, all eyes were on me as if I had just caught them doing something they shouldn't have.

"So, who wants to tell me what the hell is going on with all of you?" I asked, crossing my arms.

"Why do you think there's anything wrong?" Brayden asked, looking slightly guilty.

Shrugging my shoulders, I walked over to the couch. "I didn't, but now I know there is, and the fact that you have been shielding me from your emotions all day tells me it's something I'm not gonna like."

"It's not something you need to worry about or fix," Micah grumbled, turning to look out the window.

"Right—like I'm going to believe that," I commented, managing to stop myself from rolling my eyes. "A fight between you guys is the last thing we need to deal with right now. Or did you all forget that the Dark Lord is building an army of hosts that can get through our wards without detection?"

"No, we didn't forget, Lailah," Micah snapped. "Knowing what we are dealing with is part of the problem."

Jay shot Micah a look, and they seemed to have this odd conversation through their mutual stare-down. Finally, Micah huffed and yanked on his headphones, tuning us all out. Jay got up and sat next to me, waiting a moment to make sure he had my full attention.

"When we get back, things are going to change," Jay stated. "I know that Beth had a plan for what Elementi education to start with, but the way things are going, we need to fast-track you."

"I agree. Learning all I can about demons and how we can all work together best is what we need to focus on."

Jay nodded his head, happy with my answer. Leaning back, he rested his head against my shoulder and shut his eyes, surprising me with his causal approach to physical contact. It seemed that the more that Jay opened up to me, the easier things like this became for him to do. Having had the *honor* of meeting his father, I knew that outward expressions of love and affection were not something that happened often in his family, if ever. Moments like these showed me just how much we needed each other to get through this, because none of us were strong enough to do it on our own.

Brayden reached out and took my hand in his, rubbing his thumb over the back of my hand. "Angel, I need you to know that I'm not keeping secrets from you. If I felt like you needed to know what was going on, I would tell you. There are some things, as men, that we need to work through ourselves. Sharing a significant other with four other people is bound to result in some disagreements."

Letting out a sigh, I leaned my head back and turned so I could look at him. "I understand that, I do, but working as a team is the only way that we will survive this. When we have that split second to make a choice, knowing that you guys will trust me to do as I ask is everything. Can you say without a shadow of a doubt that if Parker called to run, or freeze, you would trust that he is making the right call?"

Brayden looked at me, and I could see him truly taking what I was saying to heart. He didn't answer me, but somehow I knew he wouldn't, because I already knew the answer—he wouldn't listen to Parker. While they had been making their plans for when we got back, so had I. They only saw things from the standpoint of protecting me and keeping me out of harm's way, but they needed to know other people's lives were at stake too. The Dark Lord had made it clear that he was going to do whatever he could to pull me to his side, even if that meant breaking me in the cruelest way possible. Not to mention, the whole serum and venom issue. I couldn't even guess how this was going to turn out.

The rest of the flight back to school was quiet, and Hudson slept soundly, to the point that I had to go back and wake him up when it was time to land. He looked much more himself, and the lost look he'd given me had left his eyes.

When we de-boarded the plane, I was almost knocked over by a speeding dart of lime green hair. "Lala," Cami yelled as she wrapped her arms around me. "You can never leave me that long again. You get into way too much trouble to be trusted with just these idiots to watch out for you."

Laughing, I hugged her back just as tightly, having missed her just as much. "I think you might be right."

Giving me a broad smile, Cami linked arms with me and pulled me towards the car that was going to take us back to school. Cami refused to leave my side, so she sat in the very back of the SUV with me and made one of the boys drive.

"I've had to go weeks without seeing her, so you all are just going to have to deal," Cami grumbled.

The boys didn't really argue and loaded into the vehicle heading back to the Manor. As much fun as it had been to travel, I was so very ready to be back in my own space. Cami chattered as we drove, filling me in on all the happenings of the school and her break thus far.

"So now we need to go shopping," Cami declared.

"Wait, what?" I blurted.

Rolling her eyes at me, Cami pouted. "I knew you weren't really listening to me, Lala. I was saying that we need to go and get outfits for the New Year's party in town. Everyone goes. It's the highlight of winter break."

"You can't take her, you little gremlin. I already asked Trouble to go with me," Parker announced.

Snapping my gaze to his, I blinked. "You did?"

Parker gasped and clutched his heart. "Trouble, I'm

wounded you can't remember. I asked you before you left for Brayden's."

"I'm sorry. With everything that's happened, it must have slipped my mind, but since no one else has asked me to do anything, then I will happily go with you to the party," I answered, knowing I couldn't turn Parker down.

With everything going on, he was the one person I hadn't spent that much alone time with, and that needed to change. Knowing him and his love for attention and parties, this sounded like something he would really enjoy doing.

"Is this like prom? Do we need to coordinate colors?" I asked, having limited experience and never having gone out on New Year's Eve.

Cami burst out laughing. "Lala, you kill me, you sweet, innocent thing, you. No, this is a time to knock 'em dead with your killer looks and guarantee you get a kiss once the clock strikes midnight."

Micah whipped around in his seat, glaring at Cami. "You better not let her buy anything that would make her look like a hooker. I know you, Camilla."

Cami lunged forward, forgetting that we had a row of people blocking her from getting to Micah. "I dare you to fucking call me that to my face, buttmunch. Do you really think that I would let my darling Lala out of the house like that?"

"Just know that I will hold you personally responsible if it happens, and then we will see just how tough you are," Micah challenged.

Parker's mischievous grin was back in full force for the first time today. "I say we have a match between the two of you and finally let you guys at each other, settle this once and for all."

"I like the sound of this," Cami said, perking up at the idea. "Remember, no fucking powers allowed with the normal human."

Micah gave her a smirk before he turned back to the front. "Don't worry, I won't need them to beat your ass."

"Big words, flame boy. Better hope they don't bite you in the ass when I win," Cami taunted, winking at me.

Shaking my head, I looked out the window as we pulled back onto the school grounds, letting this happy moment wash over me and knowing it wouldn't last.

CHAPTER 17

LAILAH

We all agreed to take the next day off since this whole winter break had been a crazy whirlwind of one thing after another. Beth did have us sit down with her and a few others of the Elementi leadership to go over what we learned while we were gone, wanting to hear it firsthand. I was surprised to see how many people were not at all bothered by what was going on in the labs, instead saying it had brought us information we wouldn't have had otherwise. To me, that was hardly a good enough reason to allow such a thing to continue happening, but to them we were still children who didn't understand the world and how it was a necessary evil. Thankfully, we didn't need to work with them on a regular basis, and Beth was our go-between for other matters.

"Lailah, I have to agree with the boys. We need to get you educated on matters we are dealing with at the moment. Once things calm down, we can go back and deal with the history of our people since it is important to know where we came from," Beth said, sitting across from me in her office, looking up from her tablet.

Beth and I had spent the past hour working on a new

schedule for the upcoming semester. It looked like I wouldn't be doing any classes on the main campus, instead doing all the work here in the Elementi headquarters under the Manor.

"Will it draw attention that I'm here on campus but not taking classes?" I asked, looking up from the list of classes the Elementi offered.

"Hmm, I'm just afraid if we even did one class on campus like Jay, it might make things even more obvious. If we keep you out of sight, then people will talk less, assuming you left the campus," Beth reasoned.

Something about that didn't sit well with me. I didn't want any of those girls who had it out for me to think they won. "Even if I am Synergy, I would still like to graduate with a degree of some kind."

"Oh, you will. Even if you are taking Elementi classes, you will graduate with a Masters in Mythology and Ancient History," Beth informed me. "I guess you could also add on something for the amount of martial arts that you will be learning as well, but we don't typically do that since it's not on the main catalog of class options," Beth mused, tapping her chin with a pen.

I shook my head and looked over the list I'd written down for this semester. "Okay, so if we do Intro to Religion and Demonology, Elemental Powers 101, Basic Hand-to-Hand Combat, Weapons Training, along with Wards and Spells Against Demons, that should cover what I need to know right away."

"Don't forget the special sessions we are going to do with Nona and Tony to see what we can do with your combined powers," Beth interjected.

"Tony? You mean the security guard?" I asked, remembering him from my very first day of school.

Beth paused her typing to look up at me. "You've met?"

"Yeah, Cami sent him to help me with my boxes when I first got to school. He said they were friends, and now that makes a whole lot more sense, knowing he's part of the Elementi," I said with a shrug of my shoulders.

"Cami had the head of security for the whole school come and help you move in? I don't know why I'm even shocked at this, to be honest. I mean, of course she would do that—she never wanted to keep any of this a secret from you in the first place," Beth muttered, shaking her head. "Wild child, that one. Let's hope Maggs can manage to handle her crazy."

I had my money on Maggs dealing with Cami's brand of crazy with ease. The more time I spent with those two, the more I couldn't have picked a better match for my pint-sized best friend.

"Anyways, yes. Tony and Jay will be working with you on all physical aspects of your training. Nona will be in charge of anything to do with your powers, Mr. Creed will be your resource for all things demon, and Mr. Phillips for history and religion. Always feel free to reach out to me as well if you aren't sure who to ask about something. We have so many available resources that I'm sure I can find someone to help you." Beth smiled and stood up, letting me know that our meeting was over.

"Thanks Beth." I nodded, returning her smile as I left her office.

Heading back up to my room, I found Parker sitting on the couch playing some video game that had lots of shooting and explosions.

"Come on! Seriously dude, how could you play dirty like that?!" Parker yelled at the TV, tossing his control up in the air.

It was then I realized he was wearing a headset and actually talking to someone on the other end.

"I told you they would have that part of the warehouse rigged with explosives, but you still pushed me anyway. So not cool, man," Parker grumbled as the screen showed the count-down before he could log back in.

Smiling to myself, I walked past him and headed for my room, but a hand wrapped around my wrist and I was pulled onto his lap, causing me to let out a yelp.

"Hey man, I'm gonna log off for the day. It seems I've found myself some other Trouble to get into," Parker said with a wide grin and a wink, making me blush. I could hear someone talking on the headset before Parker yanked it off and pulled me more snugly against him. "What do you say you and I go into town and get some sugar cookies?"

"Really?" I asked, turning to see his face better.

"Really, really. You and I haven't had much time to ourselves, and I'm craving some quality time with my girl," Parker answered, giving me a squeeze. "It's too cold to take the bike, but I don't think you've had a ride in my pride and joy yet, have you?"

I frowned up at him. "Since I have no idea what you're talking about, I would say no. I didn't even know you had something other than your bike here."

"Oh, this is gonna be fun. Alright, go get bundled up so we can enjoy the town in all its winter glory," Parker directed, setting me on my feet and giving me a small shove in the direction of my room.

Glancing over my shoulder, I saw him vault out of the chair and race off to his room. Grinning, I headed to my closet and looked through my hoodies grabbing one that said *any time is cookie time*, pulling it on before grabbing my lighter winter jacket. Since Cami had made fun of me for my puffy winter coat, I just couldn't wear it without thinking about looking like the marshmallow creature of the *GhostBusters* movie. Snagging my floppy beanie from my suitcase that I hadn't totally unpacked, I raced out the door and down the stairs to pull on my boots, which were by the back door. Parker was there waiting for me, grabbing the keys off the hook and opening the door for me.

Heading to the garage, we stopped in front of a large truck

that was cherry-red and lifted so high that I wasn't sure how I was going to get into the thing. Parker opened the passenger door, picked me up by my hips, and tossed me into the vehicle. I laughed as I grabbed the handle to make sure I didn't fall back and slid onto the soft cloth seat. This was something I expected to see back home with all the farmers and ranchers around, not here on the other side of the world, but it totally fit Parker. Climbing in, he turned the key, and the whole thing rumbled to life, letting out a puff of black smoke like a dragon waking up from a slumber.

"Trouble, this is Roxy. My dad and I rebuilt her together when I first got my license. I thought it was high time the two of the most important women in my life, besides my mother, should meet," Parker announced.

After a few moments, we pulled out of the garage and headed into town. I'd always liked Drittilyn and how quaint it was, but add snow and Christmas decorations, and it was straight out of a picture you would find on a Christmas card. The shops looked so cheerful with the ribbons, evergreen, and shimmering ornaments that I couldn't help but smile. Parker found a spot at the end of town furthest from where we wanted to go, a not-so-subtle plan to keep us out longer. Opening my door, I waited for Parker to round the truck so I could use him to get down. Resting my hands on his shoulders, I felt his hands wrap around my hips, guiding me down as I slid from my seat.

"Did you do that on purpose so you would have to manhandle any girl you let in or out?" I asked with raised brow.

Parker looked back at the truck, then me, with a surprisingly soft expression. "You are the first woman to ever ride in Roxy. I don't even think all the guys have ridden in her before. When I say that truck is important to me, I mean that. So no, this is not some chick-mobile, if that's what you're thinking."

I was so shocked my mouth fell open, unable to come up with something to say. Taking my hand, Parker threaded his fingers between mine, and we headed off down the street. We had a blast popping in and out of random little shops, and of course Parker needed to stop by his favorite candy place and get a one-pound bag full of sweets.

"I can't believe you haven't had a Kinder egg before. They're the best. You get candy and a prize all in one," Parker said, walking backwards so he could look me in the face. "If you're willing to share some of your cookies with me, then I will gladly give you a Kinder egg all of your own—I'll even let you keep the prize."

"You drive a hard bargain, Parker. I'll have to see you eat one to show me that it's worth giving up one of my treasured sugar cookies," I teased.

Parker gaped at me, clutching his chest. "You doubt my word? Don't you know by now that I would never steer you wrong, Lailah?"

"Of course I trust you, silly, but I still don't know if your taste in sweets is compatible with mine. This could be a make-it-or-break-it moment for us," I answered sarcastically.

Parker stopped suddenly, and I crashed into him as he quickly wrapped his arms around me, holding me safely against his chest. Peering up at him, I was shocked to see that he had a worried look in his eyes. "Lailah, do you trust me? I'm not talking the way you trust a friend. I mean, do you truly trust me enough to give a piece of your heart to me?"

Taken aback by this dramatic turn of events, I couldn't seem to answer him right away. Seeing my hesitation, an expression of hurt flickered across his face, and he leaned down, resting his forehead against mine, taking a few deep breaths. After a moment, he released me and took a step back, turning to head down the street.

"Wait, Parker," I blurted, grabbing his coat to keep him from walking away from me. "I do trust you. I'm sorry I hesitated, but you caught me off guard, so I froze. Ever since the first day I met you, you have been nothing but kind, caring, and understanding. Any time I have been unsure or too scared to try something, you are right there by my side to help me through it, and then the first to celebrate with me when I discover something new. I wouldn't have been able to get this far without you—so to answer your question, yes, I do trust you."

Parker turned back to me and brushed his thumb along my cheek. "You don't trust me the way *I* want you to—hell, *need* you to—but maybe someday I'll prove to you that you can." Wrapping an arm around my shoulder, he pulled me against his side as he opened the door to Anne's bakery. "Come on, Trouble. We have some sugar cookies to buy."

CHAPTER 18

PARKER

I watched as Lailah and Anne talked, catching up after being gone for the holidays. The soft smile on Lailah's face made my heart melt just a little, especially after everything she had gone through the past week or so. I was glad to be home and to get some sense of normalcy back.

I knew that she would be starting classes and training full time soon, so I pounced on the chance to spend time with her alone. Sitting back and watching her bond with the others was a double-edged sword. I knew we had a solid connection, but it wasn't the kind I wanted. Fear creeped in, telling me that I was nothing more than a friend to her and even if I offered up my Oath, she wouldn't take it. Sure, we had made out, but giving in to physical urges was easy—I should know.

Before I met Trouble, I'd always searched for the next emotional high. Being the Knight gifted with the power of emotions made it easy to get lost in them when I was at a party. The fun was intoxicating, pushing me to find more places I could get my next hit, so I did. Soon, I had the reputation of being a social whore who was only interested in a good time, not a long time. Which wasn't always true, I had a long time girlfriend in high school. That is until she walked away from me because she didn't think her parents would approve. Maybe that's why I decided it would be easier not to get attached, a heart as big as mine made the pain of rejection ten times worse.

Then, I crashed into the one woman who gave me the biggest jolt of emotion I'd ever experienced. Once I'd met Lailah, I couldn't seem to stay away from her. She was a light that I was drawn to, and once she came into her power, the pull was even stronger.

When we fought against Ms. Tabitha back in Austria, the rush of having her pull and push power through me was unlike anything I had ever felt before. I couldn't even imagine what it would look like when we Bonded and she could feel my emotions the same way I felt hers when we touched. Knowing she would have five different people's emotions rolling around in her brain made me worry. Being a person who could pick up on that with a simple touch if I was trying, I knew how over-whelming it could be not knowing if you're the one feeling it or not.

"Parker, oh Parker," Lailah called in a sing-song voice. "Earth to Parker, you still with me?"

Shaking myself out of my thoughts, I slapped my customary grin on my face. "Aw, you can't get rid of me that easily, Trouble. What's up?"

"Well, I didn't know how many cookies you wanted or if you liked them frosted or not," Lailah said, pointing at the case.

Walking up, I settled my hands on her hips and rested my head on her shoulder, looking at the options. "What are you feeling like today Trouble?"

"Oh, I always want the plain kind. The frosting covers up the taste of the cookie too much," Lailah answered, turning her head to look at me.

"Then we will take all you have left, Ms. Anne," I declared, looking up at the older woman who had a knowing smile on her face.

Lailah gasped and turned to face me. "Parker, that is far too many. We can't eat all of them today."

"We'll see about that. I know a few others who might be interested in getting one of your cherished cookies." I winked.

I smiled even more as her cheeks bloomed with a soft blush and her eyes dropped from mine as she smacked my arm. "Don't you dare start *that* again. If you and Cami keep talking about my favorite food like that, I won't be able to look at it the same."

"Oh, Trouble, I haven't been able to think of a sugar cookie the same way since the first time I met you," I teased as I looked up at Ms. Anne. "I don't know if you remember me at all, but I was the asshole who smashed her cookie the first time she came here."

Ms. Anne chuckled. "As it so happens, I do remember you were quite upset that you had ruined your chances with this young lady."

"Look at us now, only a few months later and we're dating. Guess you could say your cookies brought us together." I sighed, hugging Lailah tight against my chest as she muttered something under her breath. "So it's only right that we need to have all the cookies you have for our date."

"Very well, I'll box them up for you." Ms. Anne smiled, pulling the tray out of the display and carrying it into the back where I guessed there might be more.

Lailah pushed back from my chest so she could look up at me. "What on earth are we going to do with that many cookies? For real," she demanded, giving me an attempt at a glare.

"I already told you not to worry about it, but we have one more stop to make before we head off to our second location," I explained, knowing that spontaneity was not her strong suit.

She just rolled her eyes at me and let herself relax against my chest as we waited for Ms. Anne to come back. It didn't take long, and I was a little surprised at the large pastry box she brought back out with her.

"Now, I do have to admit I would love to know what you're going to do with thirty cookies, but I'm sure Lailah will fill me in another time," Ms. Anne said as she rang up the purchase and took my card.

I ignored Lailah's groan at the price, but she was just going to have to learn that I liked to spoil her, as did a few of the other men in her life. Having seen from past experience what Brayden was like with previous girls he had around him, I couldn't wait to see Lailah lose her shit when he did something over the top and romantic. Even Micah, for the dick he was, had been known to splurge on a girl or two. He might not have much of a heart left inside his chest, but what he did have was some smooth moves when he wanted to.

Holding the box like it was made of glass, I headed out of the bakery, holding the door open for Lailah. "We need to head down to the shop at the end of the street for the last item before we can head out of town."

"Did you really have this all planned or are you just pulling this out of your ass?" Lailah questioned as we headed off.

"What answer would give me better chances of making out with you later?" I grinned.

Shaking her head, Lailah laughed, and it was the most soothing sound to my soul.

"Just because you said that, I'm not going to on principle, but I might be willing to let you change my mind."

"Oh, you're in trouble. You can't lay down a challenge like that and not expect me to kick its ass," I said, bumping into her with my hip and wagging my brows before coming to a stop next to a small chocolate shop. "This is our next stop. Would you mind holding these while I get what we need?"

Gently, I transferred the box to her and pulled the door open for us. This was one of my favorite places. The owner was a grizzled old man who was training his son to take over the business when he died, but that was twenty-five years ago, and he was still here every day making his delicious chocolate with secret recipes.

"Would you look at what the cat dragged in," Hugo grumbled as he shuffled his way to the counter. "If you're looking for the raspberry drops, I told you I only make those in season, and now is not when that happens. Don't even try that smooth talking mumbo jumbo with me. I won't be swayed to use that greenhouse, chemically treated shit they have in the stores."

I couldn't hold back my bark of laughter as I saw Lailah's shocked face at how this man was talking.

"Calm down, old man, I'm not here to harass you. The smack on the hand with that wooden spoon of yours isn't quickly forgotten. I am in need of a container of your famous hot chocolate that has the super secret recipe," I explained.

Hugo narrowed his eyes at me, his bushy eyebrows almost hiding them from view. "You wouldn't be sassing me now, would you boy? What kind of business owner would I be if I handed every Tom, Dick, and Harry my recipes? This is why I can't let Lucas take over—too soft, that one, but Anna is off in London running some bigwig's company when she would have been better off here with her family."

"You know that if you want to retire, you have to let Lucas take on more responsibility at some point," I pointed out, knowing what his answer would be.

Hugo slammed his large fist on the wooden counter. "Do I look like I need to retire to you, boy? I'm not going soft any time soon like all those others in their rocking chairs. Bah, when you stop working is when you die." Shaking his head, he looked up and seemed to notice Lailah for the first time. "Why didn't you tell me you brought a lady friend with you? Letting me go on rambling like some old dodder."

Shuffling his way around the counter, he walked up to

Lailah, took the box from her hands, and shoved it into mine. "Ladies should never carry things if a man is around, you hear me? Don't let this runt fool you into taking care of him; I know full well that he is more than capable. You see, his family and mine go way back, been knowing this idiot since he was a baby. If he ever needs some straightening out, you let me know and I'll take care of it." He patted Lailah on the cheek, giving her a rare smile.

"Hey now, don't you be trying to steal my girlfriend like that," I challenged.

Hugo looked at me, then grunted. "Don't make it so easy and I won't. Now, you said you need hot chocolate. I'm guessing you need it to keep her around when she realizes what she agreed to date. I'll make up for the large thermos, then. It's gonna take quite a bit."

Without too much more hassle, hot chocolate in hand, Lailah and I headed back to the truck, where I got to help her once again up into her seat. As we drove, the silence between us was comfortable and easy, something I've never really been able to experience with anyone else before. It was more my nature to be on the move, ready for the next thing to happen, but Lailah made me appreciate what was happening now.

Back on the school property, I took her over to the Computer Science building, where I spent most of my time focusing on my major. Waving my key card over the sensor, I opened the door to my space and heard her gasp.

Taking her hand, I carried the cookies and handed her the cocoa as I led her into my sanctuary. My freshman year I'd been able to sweet talk one of the professors into letting me have my own office if I did extra work for the school when they needed it. My first year here, I built my own computer and set it up in this room, turning the whole thing into the perfect nerd den. My black and purple racer chair sat waiting for me to take my place in front of the three large screens and wield the power of the internet at my fingers. The box that held the brains of my computer had glass sides so you could see everything working. LED lights set it aglow, dancing along to whatever music I was playing. Even my keyboard lit up in rainbow colors, adding life to the room. On the walls were posters of my favorite video games and diagrams of the first microprocessor chip and other computer-related technology.

"Parker, where are we?" Lailah asked, taking it all in.

Turning, I splayed my arms out. "This, Trouble, is my nerd-dom on display. Here is where I perform the magic—well, okay, lately I've just been sneaking in here to play video games, but don't tell the staff that or they'll take away my keycard."

"This is so cool! Are we going to play something together?" she asked, taking a seat in my chair.

"What a silly question, of course we are. I know how pitiful your video game knowledge is, so we are going to start chipping away at that. Now, have you ever heard of a game called W.O.W.? And how do you feel about being an elf?" I asked as I pulled in another chair from the main room.

"Um…"

I let out a heavy sigh. "We have a lot of work to do. Good thing we have the cookies and hot chocolate to fuel us through this."

CHAPTER 19

LAILAH

"Lala, come on. You haven't been able to spend any time with me since you got back," Cami whined, sprawled across my bed. "I have this whole day planned out. I just need you to come with us."

Maggs sat in one of the armchairs in my room, looking at her girlfriend with a raised eyebrow. "If you keep acting like that, no one will want to hang out with you."

Cami shot up and looked at her, wide-eyed. "Even you?!"

"How 'bout you stop being so needy and we just don't find out, okay?" Maggs suggested as she turned to me. "We do really have a fun day planned and would love to have you join us."

"It's still winter break, and you have been working the WHOLE time," Cami pointed out, her face so hopeful.

"Fine. I was going to get some reading done, but you're right. It could wait a little longer," I sighed, giving in.

Cami shot off my bed, hooting and hollering while doing this odd little dance. "Alright, now you have to dress warm. We're gonna be outside. I'm gonna get snacks from Sarah and meet you downstairs when you're ready."

It didn't take me long to pull on some extra layers and thick wool socks, beating them to the door. Cami arrived with a basket filled with goodies for us to eat wherever we ended up. Thankfully, Maggs pulled up in her SUV and we piled in, not having to cram into Cami's little Fiat. Chatting as we drove, the time flew by until we were pulling down a dirt road that was easy to find with all the other vehicles that had made the journey. We ended up in an open field with a large pond with people ice skating on it.

"Guys, are we really going ice skating?" I asked excitedly.

"As long as you promise not to show me up, because something about your reaction tells me you've done this before," Cami laughed, seeing me almost bouncing in my seat.

"I love ice skating, but I haven't been able to talk anyone into going with me, and it's not fun when you're by yourself." I grinned, clapping my hands. "This was such a great idea, Cami."

"Now you're getting in the spirit! And you wanted to stay home and *read*. This is why you need me in your life, otherwise you would miss out on all the fun stuff ," Cami announced as she hopped out of the car.

We headed to the little wooden hut where they were renting the skates, and soon we were on the ice. My family wasn't big into sports, but hockey was one that Kyle played, so I got to take figure skating while he had practice. Once I discovered my love for track, though, that fell by the wayside. After a few steps, the feeling of it came back to me as if I'd never taken time off. Cami was a little more unsteady, but a few laps around the pond and she was skating circles around me. I was glad that there weren't many people out today, meaning we didn't have to fight for space on the ice. When we were ready to take a break, Cami slipped off her skates and grabbed the snacks from the car.

"Thank you so much for doing this, Cami. It's been one of the best days," I said as she handed me hot chocolate. "Holy shit. This stuff is amazing."

"Right? There is this old man in town who makes it. It's

ruined all other hot chocolate for me for the rest of my life," Cami said, hugging her cup.

"I thought it might be from there, Parker took me the other day," I shared as I savored the chocolaty goodness.

Our peaceful moment was cut short as a woman screamed, drawing our attention back to the lake. There stood a man, his hair wild, clothes torn and disheveled, holding a little boy in his arms with a knife to his throat. It took me a moment to realize he was also on the end of the pond that had thinner ice and had been marked off by cones.

"Oh, Synergy. Come out, come out, wherever you are. I would hate for something awful to happen to this little boy," the man said as he dissolved into crazed laughter.

I tossed aside my drink and rushed towards the pond without even a second thought. I could hear Cami and Maggs hot on my heels, refusing to let me deal with this on my own.

No, no, no. This couldn't be happening right now.

The Dark Lord had warned me that something was going to happen and that others would be affected by it, but I didn't think this was how it was going to happen. What reason would this possessed man have to harm an innocent child?

When I reached the lake, I had to slow down and carefully make my way across the ice now that I was back in my normal shoes.

"What a good little Knight you are, rushing to the rescue of this poor boy," the man said, his eyes wild and his grin manic. "Oh goody, you have friends with you! This is going to be so much more fun!"

Sliding to a stop a few feet before him, I lifted my hands, motioning him to stop as he took another step backwards. "Wait," I begged. "Please, just tell me what you want. You have my full attention. There is no reason to do anything to that child."

Panic pulsed through my veins, unsure of what I could possibly do.

"What I want... hahaha. Synergy, this has nothing to do with me. I am but a humble servant of the Dark Lord," he said with pride. "Did you know that I responded to the serum so well that I don't need to be taken over by another? He said that I was dark enough all on my own. Can you imagine that? As a now *enhanced* human with my inhibitions taken away, I am evil enough to rival a demon."

It was no secret there were dark and evil people in the world that did horrible things, but to be face to face with one such person was not something I had planned on experiencing. "Who are you? If we are making introductions, it only seems fair I know who you are."

"Marvin Brown is who I was, but now I was given the name Ubel by the masters I serve, to match the evil that lives inside of me," he answered, giving a slight bow and causing the little boy to whimper.

"So, Ubel, tell me what happens now?" I questioned.

Ubel gave me a smile that was more teeth than anything as he took another step back and slammed his heel into the ice, shattering a hole. "The Dark Lord wants to remind you that all that is to come is your doing. Their blood will be on your hands as much as mine, Synergy. The only way to make it stop is to kill me or surrender before the body count becomes too high."

Before I could even react, Ubel dropped the boy into the icy water with a shriek and disappeared in a puff of tell-tale demonic green smoke. Bolting forward, I slipped, slamming my knees against the ice, but I didn't care as I scrambled as fast as I could to the hole. The surface had already started to freeze again, so I punched it with my fist, pulling the shards of ice out of my way. Cami and Maggs were beside me doing the same, but we all paused as the ice groaned under our combined weight.

"You need to back up. The ice can't handle the three of us," I snapped as I thrust my arms into the water, trying to see if I could grab the boy. "How deep is this pond?"

"This is the deepest part. More than six feet, close to ten," Maggs answered as she scooted back slightly, Cami less willing to listen.

There's no other option if I'm going to save this boy. I have to go after him; the water is too dark to see anything.

Peering over my shoulder, I saw Cami's wide eyes lock on the opening. Before she could stop me I dove headfirst into the water. Calling my power to the surface, I threw it out around me, lighting up the murky water with its golden glow. It gave me enough light that I could see the little boy below me. Using all my strength, I swam as fast as I could, even as my skin burned against the frigid water.

Reaching out, I grabbed his little hand and pulled him close to me. I was able to use the bottom of the pond to push off, giving me momentum as I struggled to swim back to the surface. I prayed that I would be able to find the opening as I felt my lungs burning with the need for oxygen. As my limbs grew heavy and it was even more of a struggle to keep moving forward, a hand appeared. Reaching up, I brushed the fingertips of the person, causing them to dart towards me and grasp my wrist. Knowing we were saved, I gave everything I had to kick up the last few inches so other hands could grab hold of us and drag us out of the water. Gasping for air and coughing, I rolled onto my side as the boy was pulled from my arms. People were frantically shouting and moving around me, but I was so cold it was all I could focus on.

Cami's face loomed over me, her face tight with fear and anger. "What the fuck were you thinking, Lailah?! You could have died pulling a stunt like that! Hell, you still could if we don't get you warmed up."

They both grabbed me and hauled me up, moving to the closest bank instead of crossing the pond like we did before.

Once we were on solid ground, they moved as quickly as they could, dragging me towards the SUV.

"The boy," I croaked, fighting against them. "Did he make it?"

Maggs glanced down at me as she threw open the car door and set me in the passenger seat. Ignoring me, she ran around to start the truck, turning the heat up as high as it could go. Cami started pulling off all my clothes, chucking them into the back of the SUV, muttering to herself still.

"Cami," I pressed as she yanked my sodden shirt over my head. "I need to know—did the boy live? Is he alright?"

Frowning, she glanced over in the direction of the pond but still wouldn't talk to me. I tried to turn so I could see what was going on since Cami wouldn't tell me anything, but she stopped me, cupping my face between her hands.

"Please trust me, Lala. Just look at me. We need to get you warm. You are literally turning blue right before my eyes," she begged, wrapping a blanket around me that Maggs pulled from the back seat. "I can't answer your questions because I don't know. They started giving him CPR right away, but other than that, I don't know. As your guardian, you are my first priority."

My body started to shake, and not just from the cold, as I processed her words. "What if I didn't save him in time? It would be my fault he's dead. I... I could have stopped this from happening, but I refused."

Cami grasped my shoulders and gave me a rough shake. "You listen to me, Lailah—none of this is your fault. There was a crazy man who admitted he was evil and twisted. You are not responsible for someone else's actions. He came here knowing he was going to hurt someone to mess with your head. This is exactly what the Dark Lord wants to have happen, and we can't let him win—do you hear me?"

Numb, I nodded my head, but I didn't really believe what she was saying to me. I chose to taunt the Dark Lord in our last conversation, and he was making good on his threat in a more twisted way than I could have imagined. *Was this just the beginning?*

"I need to get you back home so we can warm you up. The last thing we need is for you to be out of commission when you are the key to dealing with all of this crazy shit," Cami muttered as she tucked me into the seat and buckled me.

Maggs hopped into the driver's seat as Cami pulled out her cell that had been going off like crazy. "Hudson, we have a situation. Lailah is hypothermic after taking a swim in the ice-skating pond. I have her out of most of her wet clothes and wrapped in a blanket with the heat on. What else should we do while I'm heading back to you?"

I could hear Hudson talking quickly and shouting at someone, but I couldn't make out his words.

"Fuck, I'm such an idiot... I have hot chocolate I can give her... small amounts at a time... got it." Cami nodded as she hopped back out of the car and ran to the bench we had been sitting on when this all started.

She was still talking on the phone, but from the anger clouding her face, I didn't think it was Hudson she was talking to anymore. Shouting into the phone, she hung up and swore before getting back in.

"Alright, Lala. I need you to hold onto this thermos and take small sips of the hot chocolate. Don't guzzle it down—that could make you throw up," Cami instructed.

As we pulled out, I turned to get a clear view of the pond and saw the mother of the small boy cradling her son, whose arms were tightly wrapped around her neck. I'd managed to save him in time; now I had to pray they could get him to the hospital in time to keep him that way. He had been in the water longer than I had, and my whole body burned as it started to warm up.

Clasping the thermos as tightly as I could, trying to keep my hands from shaking so badly, I took a sip but spilled half of it down my chin. After the third try, I gave up and clutched the warm container to my chest, leeching any warmth I could from it. My head pounded, and all I wanted to do was close my eyes and go to sleep, but something told me that wasn't a smart idea. Staying awake until I was back at the Manor with the rest of my guys was a safer option. Between the five of them, they would know what to do once I was allowed to rest.

Maggs pulled up right in front of the house, and seconds later the guys came pouring out. Micah was the first to my door, yanking it open. Then Brayden stepped in, unbuckled me, and pulled me into his arms.

He was so warm I couldn't help but nuzzle my face against his neck, making him hiss at the contact. "Jesus fucking Christ! You're colder than an ice cube, Angel."

"Quick, we need to get her up to the bathroom and put her in the tub. One of us will have to be in there with her. I'm surprised she hasn't passed out already with the shock her body has been through," Hudson instructed as we headed up the stairs.

"Where the hell do you think you're going, Camilla?" Micah snapped.

"Don't pull this shit on me right now. I need to make sure my best friend is going to be okay," Cami challenged.

Micah let out a harsh laugh. "Like hell you are. Haven't you done enough? Let us deal with this and we'll keep you updated. Now GO."

The next thing I knew, I was being lowered into a tub full of water, crying out at the fire that surged through my body. Arms wrapped around me from behind, pulling me against a chest.

"Too hot, it hurts," I whimpered.

A different hand gripped mine and I could feel the pain lessening to be a little more bearable, letting me know that Parker was trying to help. Even then it still burned against my skin like I was set on a bed of hot coals.

"Give it a moment, Angel. The water is warm at best, but

you're so cold it must feel like we're putting you in an oven. Try to breathe through it. I've got you," Brayden comforted as he placed gentle kisses down my neck and on my shoulder, trying to soothe me.

"Trust us, Sunshine. Close your eyes and rest if you can. Your body has been through a lot, and we just have to give it time to warm up gradually," Hudson said, taking my hand and stroking it.

With their reassurance, I allowed myself to relax, and as I did, the pain seemed to lessen. The sounds of their voices faded into the background, and I dozed, secure in Brayden's arms.

"Can someone please explain to me what the fuck happened?" Micah growled, causing me to stir at his anger.

"Keep your voice down if you're going to stay in here. We need her to rest and recover," Hudson whispered harshly.

Micah grunted his acknowledgement. "My question still stands."

"Sounds like we had our first meeting of one of the Dark Lord's new serum soldiers," Parker mused.

The sound of something being smashed caused me to open my eyes just as Micah was pulling his fist out of the bathroom wall. I struggled to sit up, but Brayden held me tightly.

"Easy. He's fine, just upset about what happened," Brayden reassured. "He's going to punch a lot more walls if we don't get you better, so just rest. We will deal with everything later."

Watching as Hudson kicked out the rest of the guys from the bathroom, I took a deep breath and gave into the demands of my body to sleep.

CHAPTER 20
JAY

Pulling up to the pond in the middle of the night, with only a sliver of the moon out to shed any light, caused an eerie effect. As I got out of my Jeep with three others of my unit, I slipped on my night-vision goggles. Another SUV pulled up with the rest of my men.

I knew the trail would be cold here, but I had to start somewhere. Parker said the man vanished in a puff of demon smoke, a trait only mid- to higher-level demons possessed.

I signaled for my men to search the surrounding woods as I headed for the ice. Skirting around the edge of the pond, I found the section that Lailah and the boy had gone in. Putting a foot on the ice, I tested its strength. With all that had happened here, it groaned under my weight, and I knew it wouldn't hold me. Taking a deep breath, I pulled my powers forth, letting the wind swirl around me. I used it to solidify the ice by causing a freezing air current to flow over the water, creating a safe path to where I wanted to go. Now it creaked and shifted for another reason as the ice grew thicker and stronger. Finished, I waved the wind off and made my way confidently to the still slushy opening Lailah had dove into.

My mind flashed back to Lailah sitting in the tub, her already naturally pale skin tinged with blue and shaking violently against Brayden. Her whimpers as she was lowered into the tepid water the first time rang in my ears. After that, she'd shifted in and out of awareness every time we drained and added warmer water. I couldn't stand it any longer. I had to get out and do something, and finding this "Ubel" was at the top of my list.

Crouching down, I pulled out a handheld device that would detect the particles demons left behind when they used their powers. The reading showed high, beeping red and showing other numbers and information on the small screen. Thankfully, this was all being transmitted back to Elementi HQ, where they would analyze it. I was their guy if they needed information collected, but I would never understand things the way that Hudson, and even Brayden, could about this stuff. Sweeping the area, I tried to gauge if he walked out here onto the ice or if he just materialized and then grabbed the boy.

Cami said she hadn't noticed the man being there at all before as they skated, and from the description of the guy... she would have noticed. Even though I wasn't happy with how things turned out, I also knew how strong-willed Lailah could be when it came to protecting others. It was as if she magically forgot all her fear and trepidation and charged headfirst into danger. I thought it was an amazing quality, but seeing as she didn't have any of the proper training to handle things once she got in it... that's what made me worry.

"Commander Jay, we found something you should see," one of my heads called from the forest.

Looking up, I saw a light being waved in the air, showing me their location. Retreating from the ice, having gotten everything I needed, I headed over to see what they found. Taking off my night vision, I took in what my men had found as they gathered to shine their flashlights on the ground. Carved into the dirt was the symbol for Dantalion, the seventy-first demon, the Duke of Many Faces, and one of the Greater Demons that King Solomon had summoned to help build the temple. We learned about them in our demonology classes, but they had not been seen or heard from in history for centuries. Dantalion was a Greater Demon who could change its appearance at will, even its gender so that it could infiltrate the world better, spreading its evil through science and education.

"Son of a bitch," I growled, knowing that this had been left here for us to find.

The Dark Lord was playing a wicked game, and I was starting to realize we were many steps behind. This Ubel, as he was calling himself, must have been who had infiltrated the lab and stolen the serum when the time came. All the work we had been doing looking through employees was now pointless, because if this symbol was telling me what I assumed it was, we would have no idea what Ubel looked like as the newly estab-lished conduit for Dantalion. One moment it could be a man, the next a woman. We might have luck finding out who this person really was if the name he gave was true, but that didn't matter trying to find him now when he could look like a whole different person.

Pulling out my phone, I called the only person I knew who would know more about this.

"Who the hell is this and do you have any clue as to what time it is?" Mr. Creed demanded, his voice thick with sleep.

"Mr. Creed, it's Jalen Minh. I apologize for the late call, but this is an urgent matter. What do you know about the demon Dantalion?"

The sound of sheets rustling told me I had his attention. "The fact that you are an Elementi Warrior and calling me at one in the morning tells me that you're not looking for hypothetical information. Let's cut to the chase and tell me what you found."

As much as I hated working with this entitled windbag, he

was the elite mind when it came to all things demon. "Earlier today, a man using the name 'Ubel' made an appearance and caused a scene at the ice-skating pond. I came back to gather more intel since he was able to use demon smoke to vanish and found the symbol of Dantalion etched into the ground, with other minor symbols that would give him a focal point to shift to."

"Ubel, you said…" Mr. Creed muttered as I heard him typing. "Do we know anything else?"

"He was there to taunt Synergy and tell her that he was one of the first to receive the serum treatment and was given powers without needing to be a host," I explained.

"Let me guess. You think this is the man who stole the serum from the lab."

"Yes sir, I do."

"Gather any and all the data you can from the area. Sweep deeper into the woods. A human can't travel as far as a demon can, even if it's a host. There should be another location with more symbols or markings to give us a better picture of what's going on. I'll start working on what I can in regards to this name he picked and the correlation to Dantalion," Mr. Creed instructed. "Oh, and please tell me I'm finally going to get a chance to teach that girl something before she walks into a trap and dies from lack of information."

I all but growled into the phone at the way he talked about Lailah, but on the other hand, I couldn't argue with him. "I believe she will be working with you sooner rather than later, sir."

"Fine, fine. Let's hope this isn't going to be as bad as I think it is, or her crash course into this world will be quite the experience," Mr. Creed said before he hung up, leaving me with dead air.

Shoving the phone back into my pocket, I relayed the information to my men. "We need to form a grid search and sweep the whole area. Keep a lookout for anything that doesn't look like it belongs. If you find anything, make sure to document and mark the area on our maps so we can go back and look at it again in the daylight."

With that, they all scattered into the night on silent feet. This was going to take the rest of the night and even the whole rest of the day if we found what we were looking for. Pulling my phone back out, I called Hudson, knowing he would still be up.

"Were you able to find anything useful?" Hudson asked when he answered.

I grunted, knowing if the situation was different they would all be out here with me, but Lailah needed them to be close by. "I wouldn't say it's useful."

"Now is not the time for cryptic conversations, Jay," Hudson admonished.

"We found some demonic symbols that might mean this whole situation just got a whole lot harder to manage. I have consulted Mr. Creed, and we need to search the woods for any other symbols and hope they tell a different story than the one I'm coming up with at the moment."

Hudson let out a harsh breath that was almost a laugh. "What is going on, Jay? Things have never been this bad. They're getting bolder."

"Synergy is in play now, Hudson. This was always going to happen. How are things with Parker?"

"Not good, even though he tries to keep the pain level down it's still a lot, but we will manage. You do what needs to be done, and we'll hold down the fort here."

I was about to end the conversation but paused, feeling a need I'd never experienced before. "Tell Lailah I'll be back as soon as I can, and not to be mad. I'm not doing this alone."

"Let's hope she doesn't kill the messenger, but yeah, I'll make sure she knows."

"Thanks man," I said before hanging up.

It was time to go demon hunting.

CHAPTER 21

LAILAH

I slept the rest of the day and halfway through the next. Whenever I woke up, I was surrounded by my guys, nestled in the middle of them keeping me warm. There was something about this that just seemed to heal more than just my dip in the pond; it was as if this is where I'd belonged my whole life and I was catching up on the years I'd missed. Cami came to check on us from time to time, bringing me piping hot cups of chai tea, but my wakefulness didn't last long, and soon I was asleep again.

When I finally awoke feeling rested, I was alone in the bed but could feel Brayden and Hudson nearby. My body still ached, but other than that, I was much more myself and ready to get up. I needed to meet with Beth and the other Elementi members to share with them what I learned about Ubel and the danger he presented if there were more like him. Ms. Tabitha was bad enough, having been blessed with demonic power without the serum, but we had no idea what Ubel could do. I'd seen him poof out of existence, and that would definitely make catching him extremely difficult.

Heading to the closet, I pulled on soft yoga pants and a shirt that said *Wake me up when winter is over.* I added a fluffy sweater, still not able to shake that last bit of chill from my bones. Exiting my room, I found Hudson sitting in his armchair, reading a book. But the moment he saw me, the book was tossed to the side and I was wrapped up in a warm hug.

"Sunshine, you need to stop taking years off my life, pulling stunts like that," he whispered into my ear as he scattered soft kisses on my face. "Do you know how lucky you are to still be alive?"

Wrapping my arms around him, I hummed at how warm he was. "Not as lucky as that little boy. If I hadn't done what I did, he for sure would have died, and I couldn't live with that on my conscience, Hudson."

"I know. I get it, I do, but that doesn't mean I have to like it. Poor Cami has been beating herself up about the whole thing, not that Micah didn't help with that," Hudson grumbled.

Micah must have really said something awful to Cami for Hudson to be so bothered by it, or it was another sign he was embracing his emotions more and not locking them away. Either way, it told me I needed to talk to her to see if I could smooth things out. Before I could pull out of Hudson's arms to do that, I felt another warm body wrap around my back.

"How are you feeling, Angel?" Brayden asked, placing a kiss on my cheek.

"Better. Still a little chilled, but I'm sure that will go away once I'm more active and moving around," I answered with a shrug. "Hudson was just telling me I might need to check in on Cami."

Brayden let out a heavy sigh and stepped away from me, letting me free from their hold. "Let's get you something to eat before you deal with that situation."

"Where is Micah?" I asked, knowing he would be upset with me for doing something so rash.

"He's down in the training center, along with Parker, dealing with his misplaced emotions. But Tony is there keeping an eye on him and refusing to let him spar with anyone," Hudson informed me as he took my hand and led me down to the dining room.

"I'll be right back. Just gonna let Sarah know you're awake and see what we have to feed you. She's been having Garrett make a bunch of really good soups in preparation," Brayden said, giving me a wink before he headed off to the kitchen.

I sat down, but I wasn't able to relax. I hated the fact that Micah was so upset about what I'd done. "Hudson, has something like this happened before with Micah?"

"What do you mean?"

"It seems that something happened between you guys while we were in France and this situation has made it worse. I'm just wondering if he's gotten this angry before, and how you guys fixed it."

Hudson looked at me, his face softening as he felt my need to have everyone get along. "Sunshine, before you showed up, this was normal. When I say that Micah has never gotten along well with others like he has recently, I mean it. I don't think I've ever seen him spend this much time together with us in the years that I have lived here." He reached out and took my hand, giving it a squeeze. "Don't take on this burden too, Lailah."

I took a moment to think that over. Brayden had told me something similar a while ago. I guess I just hadn't believed it. The version of Micah I'd been seeing was a far cry from what was happening now, and it was making me feel unsettled.

"Alright, I have Garrett's famous chicken and rice soup for you, Angel, with some homemade bread to go with it!" Brayden announced as he walked back in with a tray of food. "I brought enough for the three of us—just taking a wild guess you haven't eaten lunch either, Hudson."

Hudson smiled at Brayden as he took the bowl of soup. "You

are correct. Like yourself, I couldn't bring myself to go far from her."

"Where's Jay?" I asked, breaking off a piece of bread.

Brayden and Hudson looked at each other before they answered me.

"He's looking for Ubel..." Brayden started.

"WHAT?!" I yelled, slamming my spoon on the table as I stood. "Why would he go looking for him on his own? He should have waited for us so that we could have his back! Do you have any idea how dangerous this guy is?"

Panic clamored in my chest as I imagined all of the horrible things that could happen to him.

"Lailah, breathe," Brayden said, pulling me back down into my chair. "He isn't alone; he took a team of his men with him. They are far better trained for a situation like this than we are at the moment. This is his job, and he's good at it. Trust that he will come back to you."

Shaking in my seat, I looked between Hudson and Brayden, feeling their total confidence in Jay and trusting that he would be fine.

"Why couldn't he wait?" I whispered, slumping in my seat.

"Do you really think he would sit around while there a crazy man out there willing to harm people just to torture you? Jay's feelings for you are just as deep as our own, and this proves it," Hudson said, his voice tinged with a slightly scolding tone. "He left once you were out of danger. I have a feeling he will be back soon. Now eat your soup while it's hot, please. We *need* you to be okay, Lailah, the same way you need us to be safe."

Nodding my head, I started in on my soup and gave a soft moan at how good it tasted. Before I knew it, I was done and pouting that it was gone. Brayden laughed at me and snagged the bowl. "Let me get you another helping. It has been a day and a half since you've eaten anything. Not surprised you're hungry."

I finished the second bowl at a slower, more normal pace, and my warm, full tummy made me sleepy once again.

"Why don't we go up and watch a movie? Or would you rather take a nap?" Hudson suggested, seeing me fighting against my eyes drooping.

"A movie sounds nice. I don't want to get back in bed, I just left it," I murmured as Brayden scooped me up and carried me upstairs.

I didn't even make it fifteen minutes into the movie, snuggled between the two of them and wrapped in a blanket. The sense of warmth and security was just too much to fight against.

"Get the fuck away from me, you slimy rat bastard!" Parker bellowed, followed by the slam of a door.

A scoff sounded close by. "Why would I waste the effort on a whipped bitch like you anyway?" Micah snapped.

Struggling out of the blanket I'd been wrapped in, I got to my feet and marched over to Micah. "What the hell is your problem? I don't care what is going on with you, that is no way to treat him or anyone else in this group!"

Micah blinked at me, his eyes wide with surprise at my verbal attack. Walking over to Parker's room, I tossed open his bedroom door, catching him with his shirt off and a snarl on his face before he realized it was me. "Trouble..."

"It would be wise for your health if you didn't tell me to butt out of this. I left it alone like I was asked, hoping you would all figure it out yourselves, but this is just getting ridiculous," I grumbled.

Turning, I looked Micah in the eye and pointed at his spot. "Sit down—please."

He gave me a heavy sigh and an eye roll as he flopped into his chair. Parker came out of his room with a shirt on and took a seat in his normal spot, while Hudson and Brayden didn't move from the couch.

"I would have liked Jay to be here, but I know he's not one to be overly sensitive about things. Now, would someone like to tell me what this tension is between you guys since France?" I asked, hands on my hips, looking at the four of them.

"You really want to know what's going on?" Micah pressed, casting a dismissive gesture towards Parker. "I don't trust Parker alone with you."

Before Parker could fly out of his chair to lunge at Micah, I stepped in front of him. "No. We are not going to handle this with violence. That is not how *we* do things." Turning back to face Micah, I tilted my head to the side as I contemplated him. "So, tell me. What would you suggest to make you more comfortable?"

"I don't know how you ever trust a playboy," Micah stated. "It wouldn't be the first time he talked a girl into leaving me for him."

"To me, he isn't a playboy," I challenged. "I've never seen him act that way or even treat me in any manner other than being sweet and caring. Besides, how can he *take* me from you when I'm with you both?"

Micah sighed, shaking his head. "His element makes him weak, and he gives into any woman who pays attention to him. Can we really ever trust that he doesn't use his powers to get what he wants from people?"

Before I could stop myself, I felt my hand connecting against Micah's cheek, the sound of the slap reverberating through the room. The anger and betrayal I saw in Micah's eyes cut me to my soul.

"I'm sorry, Micah. I shouldn't have done that. There is no excuse for lashing out at you like that. But I will not allow any of you to talk or about each other like that. We are only as strong as the weakest link, remember? You taught me that. We are a team of six, and that is how we need to function. It's not the five of you protecting me from the dangers of this world, it's all of us having each other's back and acting as one unit." I dropped to my knees in front of Micah and rested my head on his legs. "None of us will survive this if we don't, and I can't lose any of you. I wouldn't be able to live through that."

A hand rested on my head, stroking my hair gently as I started to cry.

"I hear you, Cookie Monster, but this problem is going to take some time for us to work through," Micah said in a soft voice only I could hear. "He might be the element of heart, but you are the one who holds mine. If I lose you, then there is nothing left for me to live for in this world. I promise to at least try, but that is all I can promise. He needs to do his part as well." He reached down and pulled me into his lap, wrapping me up in a bone-crushing hug, his face pressed against my neck. "Please try not to be so reckless next time, and that will help too."

CHAPTER 22

LAILAH

"Seriously, guys. I think it's safe for her to leave the house. We're just going into town. No icy water anywhere close by. We're just picking out a dress for the New Year's party," Cami said, arms crossed as she looked at the boys. "And no, you cannot come with us or it will ruin the surprise. We have one day left before the shops close for New Year's Eve, and I promise that we will make sure to keep you aware of what's going on and if there are any changes... sound fair?"

"No," Micah snapped. "Look, we have no idea when or where this Ubel guy will strike next. If he can change his face and his gender, there's no telling what could happen."

I walked up to him and grabbed his hand. "Micah, Ubel doesn't want to kill me. His goal is to push me to my limit so I give up and turn myself over to the Dark Lord. There is no way I am going back on my word when I've stood my ground so far."

"What I'm worried about, Lailah, is that you'll pull another crazy stunt and end up killing yourself this time," Micah countered.

"I promised you that I wouldn't put myself in danger, and I meant it. Cami will be there with me, along with Maggs. Both of them know twenty different ways to knock me on my ass to keep me from running into danger. So please, let us go have a girls' afternoon. I will check in with all of you every hour with pictures if that will make you feel better," I pleaded.

"Every thirty minutes, and pictures every time you change locations. Back in three hours or no deal," Jay interjected before Micah could answer.

"Deal!" I said, standing on my tiptoes and leaning over to give him a peck on the lips.

Spinning on my heel, I headed for the door before they could come up with some other reason to keep me from going out, when someone caught my wrist.

"Un-uh Trouble, you can't give one of us a goodbye kiss and not the others," Parker said, pulling me back to him.

I gave him a raised eyebrow, looking past him at the others, and saw the same expectant look on their faces. Smiling, I quickly went around, giving them all kisses before I was finally allowed to leave with Cami. Hopping into her car, we headed to pick up Maggs for our outing. It was nice to take the day and shut off all other worries and just be a normal girl.

"So, what kind of party is this, anyways?" I asked as we drove.

Cami looked over and grinned at me, far too pleased with herself in this moment. "The theme this year is *The Great Gatsby,* so it will all be glitz and glam, Lala. The roaring twenties—the golden age of Europe, full of smooth jazz and champagne to celebrate the end of the war."

Now I understood why she was so excited about this party. Anything that was over the top was right up her alley, and this was going to be something to remember, by the sound of it.

"Here's the big question... fringe or no fringe?" Cami asked as we pulled up to Maggs' sorority house.

"What are you wearing?" I deflected.

"Oh, I got myself a glitzed-out tux with short shorts and

fishnets, it's gonna be amazing! Maggs won't show me her dress, so I'll just have to wait and find out with the rest of you what it looks like," Cami whined as the woman in question slipped into the car.

Maggs frowned at Cami before giving her a kiss on her pouted lips. "Babe, if you keep whining about it, I'm going to show Lailah my dress."

"You wouldn't," Cami gasped.

"Without hesitation," Maggs said, giving me a wink.

Cami started to mutter under her breath as she pulled out of the drive but didn't say another word about it. We ended up in a part of town I hadn't seen before, but it looked like it was full of the more normal chain stores. Before we headed inside, I took a selfie with the name of the shop so the guys would know exactly where I was and that I made it there in one piece. Wasting no time, Maggs and Cami filled a dressing room with dress options, and then I was shoved in to try them on.

They had picked a little of everything—long, short, sparkle, plain—it was overwhelming. I decided I didn't want a long dress, so I bypassed those and started on the others. After ten attempts, I found the perfect dress and came bursting out of the dressing room. It was a knee-length champagne colored dress with silver and gold sequins on it in an elaborate art deco pattern. It had some slight fringe on the bottom, but nothing too overwhelming, and it clung to my body in all the right ways.

"Oh!" Maggs exclaimed, covering her mouth. "Lailah, that is magnificent."

Cami let out a whistle and wagged her brows. "As I told you from the beginning, if you swung for the right team, I would be all over that."

Maggs laughed and swatted her arm. "What am I, chopped liver?"

"Are you telling me you wouldn't want a shot with her?" Cami challenged, waving in my direction.

Tapping an elegantly painted red nail on her chin, Maggs looked me up and down. "No, you're right. I would have made a pass at her, especially in that dress."

"Now you can't be mad at me for saying it, but we all know that us ladies don't stand a chance against her brooding crew of men." Cami sighed and flopped back in her chair. "Such a loss."

"You both are nuts," I chuckled. "Alright, so this is the winner. That wasn't so bad—we finished this up in no time."

Cami popped out of her seat and grinned. "Lala, we are nowhere near done. We need shoes, jewelry, and to figure out what we're doing with your hair."

Groaning, I turned back to the dressing room, realizing this was going to be the easiest part of the day. True to her word, Cami dragged me and Maggs all over the place looking for the perfect things to make this outfit pop. Watching Maggs and Cami interact warmed my heart. They were so perfect for each other, and I could easily see the love and affection they had for one another.

It drew me back to the guys and the issues they had brought up about Parker. It had never crossed my mind that they would reject one of their own because they didn't trust him. Micah might be right that I couldn't fix this between them, but I did know that I wasn't going to add to it. I wouldn't choose and never would. To me, they were each part of a whole that fit perfectly in my life, and I needed all of them.

Once we had purchased everything, we decided we needed to go to lunch at this little hole-in-the-wall Italian pizza place.

"Okay, I can't do it anymore. You need to tell me what's going on, Lala. You have been distracted all day, even if you're trying your best not to be," Cami blurted once we had gotten our pizzas.

"You've known the guys for a long time, right?" I asked Cami.

"They're practically brothers to me. We grew up together, for the most part. Happens when your family has been part of the

Elementi for generations and you're expected to follow in their footsteps whether you want to or not," she answered with an eye roll. "What do you want to know? Everything we talk about here is between us. Scout's honor."

I fiddled with my silverware before I looked up at her. "What's the deal with none of them trusting Parker? I know Micah has never kept it a secret that he doesn't like him, but it seems like the others are starting to push him to the wayside."

Cami frowned and tilted her head slightly. "What do you mean?"

"Something happened in France, but they won't tell me what. They say it's between them to figure it out as men. Okay, well, not Jay, but his issue is he's never involved with things, so that's not surprising," I rambled.

"I know that I don't know them as well as Cami does, but there is something to be said that they are all sharing one woman. All the boys have such different personalities, they are bound to clash. So I understand them saying you can't fix the problem." Maggs held up her hand when Cami started to interject. "That being said, communication needs to be one of the top priorities with all of you. You personally might not be able to fix what is going on, but they should be able to tell you what the problem is instead of keeping you in the dark."

Cami pointed a finger at Maggs and nodded her head. "What she said."

Slumping down on the table, I hung my head. "How the hell do I get these guys to talk? When we try, it always breaks out into a fist fight or yelling match."

"Do it in the training center. That way they can get their aggression out in a controlled environment. I know Tony would be happy to help get them to stop fighting against each other. It's been his one goal since he started working with them five years ago," Cami suggested. "I wouldn't mind getting to deal with my own issues with Micah at the moment. The prick."

"That's not a bad idea. I have to start working with Tony soon anyway. I can just tell them I want them all there for my first session and then lock them in the gym until they at least tell each other what's wrong."

"Oh Lala, I love the way you think." Cami winked as she took a bite of her pizza. "Now, no more talk of boys—this is a girls only event!"

Cami made sure to give me Tony's cell number before she dropped me off back at the Manor with all my bags. I waved goodbye to Cami and headed upstairs as I texted Tony, wanting to try and deal with this sooner rather than later.

LAILAH:

Hey Tony, it's Lailah, Cami's friend you helped move in. Could I possibly ask for your help with something?

TONY:

Hey Lailah, of course I remember you. Any friend of Cami's is a friend of mine. You have me curious, what can I do to help?

LAILAH:

Cami and Micah agreed to a friendly match to see who is better. Do you think we could make a tournament so that the guys could duke it out and deal with this anger between them?

TONY:

I knew I liked you. Yeah, I think I could come up with a way to manage those two. We can do it on the 2nd when I see you for assessment.

LAILAH:

Assessment????

TONY:

Yeah, I like to see what I'm working with before I make up a training regimen. Don't worry, I promise it's nothing too crazy.

LAILAH:

Sounds good. See you later.

Heading to my room, I saw Micah's door was open and he was at his computer, headphones on, bobbing to whatever he was listening to. Catching sight of me as I passed, he tore off his headphones and ran to the door.

"Hey, you have a good time?" he asked, leaning against the door jamb.

I held up my multitude of bags and shrugged my shoulders. "Shopping isn't my favorite pastime, but it's always great to spend time with Cami and Maggs."

Micah's face scrunched up in disgust. "Yeah, I'm glad you talked me out of going with you. That would have been torture. How did you guys go to so many places in such a short amount of time?"

"Cami was on a mission, and I've learned it's better to just roll with it. But I did find the perfect outfit for the party and a few things I needed to pick up in general," I answered. "I'm gonna go put all this away and relax for a bit. She wore me out."

Micah stepped up to me and lifted a hand to feel my forehead. "You do feel a little warm. You don't think you're coming down with a cold, do you, after what happened the other day?"

Smiling at him, I leaned in and gave him a kiss, letting it linger just a little. "Who knew you could be such a sweet boyfriend."

Micah grunted as he turned me around by my shoulders and marched me to my room. "Yeah, well don't go spreading that shit around. Can't let that reputation stick after all the work I did making everyone think I'm an asshole."

"Don't worry, I'm not sure that will ever change," I teased as he took the bags from me and put them in my closet.

"Oh? And what's that supposed to mean?" Micah asked, prowling towards me with a glint in his eye.

Backing away from him, I hit the bed and sat on it, looking up at him looming over me. "Oh, just that the sweet moments are few and far between, but I kinda like that since it makes them more special."

"Not everyone can be a Brayden or a Hudson, showering you with roses and sweet words," Micah pointed out as he leaned down and nipped at my ear. "Don't you know that every woman secretly wants a bad boy to call her own? Well, Cookie Monster, here I am, ready to show you all the wicked things you never will get from your two sweet and tender lovers."

A shiver went down my spine as his words flooded me with need. I knew the moment Micah and I crossed that line I would never get enough of him. Slowly, he kissed along my jaw until he reached my lips and caught my lower lip between his teeth, pulling me to him. As I gave into him, he captured my lips, making me moan without even laying a hand on me.

All too soon, he stood up and smirked at me. "Have a good rest." And he left me all hot and bothered, not even bothering to glance back at me as I all but growled at him.

"Asshole," I yelled, throwing one of my decorative pillows in his direction.

"Every day, all day, and proud of it," he said as he closed my door.

CHAPTER 23
LAILAH

It was finally New Year's Eve, and even though the party wasn't until later, there was a lot to do. Cami and Maggs arrived in the early evening, and we started the long process of getting ready. Mind you, we were very easily distracted, talking about other things, but we managed to get the important things covered. Cami talked me into wearing my hair straight, which I don't think I'd ever done except for the few times a year I went to get my hair done at the salon. It was always so much work that I didn't have the energy to do it on my own. So, once I was out of the shower, Maggs blow dried it and started the ordeal of flat ironing it. When she was done a million years later, I was shocked to see what I looked like with my hair done and a full face of makeup.

"Aw, my baby Lala is growing up before my very eyes." Cami sniffed, wiping fake tears from her eyes.

I glared at her but then turned back to the mirror. "They better not get used to this sort of thing. I'm not cut out to be this high maintenance."

"I agree. Some things should be kept special or they lose their *wow* factor," Maggs said, giving me a wink.

"Okay, so we have an hour before we need to leave for this thing. Can I see your dress now, babe?" Cami begged, pulling out the puppy dog eyes and quivering lower lip.

Maggs just rolled her eyes and shooed us both out of the bathroom so she could get changed. My dress was in the closet, so I decided just to go ahead and put it on since Cami, having no shame, was tossing off her clothes in the middle of my room. I still couldn't get over how large this dang closet was, and I hardly had clothes to fill one row or more than four drawers out of the eight I had available to me. Do people really need that much stuff?

"Okay, everyone dressed?" Cami called. "On the count of three, we shall reveal ourselves. One... two... three."

Shaking my head, I walked out of the closet but stopped short as Cami stood there, striking a pose in her outfit for the night. The tux was blinged out to the max, and even the top hat perched on her head sparkled.

I couldn't hold back my laughter as I took her in. "Girl, you look like a burlesque dancer, or straight from a Broadway show in that getup."

"Don't be jealous, Lala. You know this is fabulous and will turn everyone's heads when we show up," Cami said, giving me a twirl.

Maggs opened the bathroom door, and Cami gasped. Her retro rockabilly girlfriend was stunning in a black tassel dress that hit mid-thigh, and with her long legs, it made it seem impossibly too short for my taste. She smirked at Cami, and when she did a twirl, all the tassels floated out in a wild dance. "What were you saying, babe, about turning heads?"

"God, I am one fucking lucky woman," Cami gushed as she pulled Maggs down for a heated kiss.

Feeling like they might need a minute, I slipped out of the bedroom and headed downstairs to find the guys. They were all hanging out in the library, and when I walked in, I thought I was at a photoshoot for *GQ* magazine or something. Each of them had on a formal tux, and even though I had seen them in one for the Christmas party, it still made my heart flutter.

Parker whistled his appreciation as he walked over. "Damn, Trouble."

My cheeks heated as I felt my blush bloom across them. He took my hand and spun me around like I was a ballerina or something, embarrassing me even more.

"Damn, I am so glad to be the one who asked you to go and get to have you on my arm all night." Parker grinned.

"You better let the rest of us have a chance to dance with her, though," Brayden said as he walked up and gave me a kiss on the forehead. "It would be torture not to be able to hold you in my arms, at least for a little while."

How could this man make my heart melt so easily?

"Of course I'll save a dance for all of you. Even if I'm Parker's date, you're all still mine," I answered with a smirk. "I better not catch some other woman getting her hands on you all."

"There's other women?" Parker asked, his brows scrunched. He tried to hold the expression as long as he could, but eventually it crumbled into laughter as he slid his arm around my waist. "I don't think you'll have to worry about that, Trouble."

Cami and Maggs finally made it down to join us, and I couldn't help but notice they both looked a little rumpled after their makeout session. "So I'm driving, right?"

"No," all the guys said loudly, making me giggle.

"Tough crowd, tough crowd." Cami frowned, hand on her hips. "Alright, what was your bright idea then, boys?"

There was a knock at the front door, and we all turned to look at it.

"That would be our plan," Micah drawled. "A limo so none of us have to drive or worry if we drink."

"Okay, flame boy. That was a good idea, I'll give you that,"

Cami said with an approving nod before clapping her hands together. "Let's get this show on the road."

Piling into the limo, we headed off to the event hall where the party was going to take place. Waiting for us was chilled champagne and glasses, which Cami promptly filled and shared with us. Lifting her glass, she shared her toast. "May this night be one to never forget and the year to come be filled with more adventure, love, and overall badassery."

Laughing, we all clinked glasses and sat back, enjoying the excitement that was filling the space as we geared up to let loose and live a little.

The whole building was lit up, making it seem like it glowed in golden light. Cars of people were being dropped off at the front of the building, so I had a few moments to take it all in. Typically with my family back in Wisconsin, we would be hanging out in the living room, watching movies and eating snack foods until the countdown. Some years, my parents would just stay up to watch the ball drop in New York and go to bed an hour early while the three of us kids stayed up for the real deal. Every once in a while, Kyle would have a girl he was dating and they would be at a friend's house, but this kind of thing was something I never dreamed of experiencing. Who knew that going to college would show me how much of the world I had been missing out on, trapped away in my own little corner of my small Midwest town?

As I exited the limo, Parker took my hand and tucked it into his elbow, pulling golden tickets out of his jacket pocket.

"Why do I get the feeling these tickets cost far more than I think they should?" I muttered as he smirked down at me.

"Nope, none of that, Trouble. You are well worth any price to spoil."

I frowned up at him. "You don't have to spend money on me for me to feel spoiled."

"Yet another reason why we love to do it. You are so very easy to please. It actually makes it fun to splurge when it's not demanded," Parker said with a shrug.

"Don't ever let me become one of those girls, please." I grimaced, horrified at the idea.

"I don't think it's possible for that to ever happen," he said as he handed over our tickets. The man at the door scanned them and gestured us through.

The hall was decked out in gold, feathers, and pearls, and in the center of the main room was the largest champagne tower I had ever seen. Buffet tables were lined on both sides with finger foods and other small delights for you to munch on, along with a full-service bar on the back wall. I could hear jazz music coming through the doors on the right and took a wild guess that's where the dancing was. Parker led me further into the room, and I couldn't help but gawk at all the women dressed to the nines and the men in their dapper suits. Now I was very glad that Cami and Maggs made me spend so long getting ready—this was not a place you could show up looking half-assed.

"Where to first?" Parker asked, turning to me. "We can eat, drink, or dance our faces off. I hear the band is the bee's knees."

I raised a brow at him with a smile tugging at my lips. "Did you look up phrases to use at this party?"

"Maybe... still, it doesn't change the question," Parker dismissed, holding out a hand to me. "Shall we? I'm not trying to brag or anything, but I have a certain talent for doing the jitterbug."

"Oh, is that what the boys are calling it these days?" Cami chirped, her face the picture of innocence.

I burst out laughing at the confused expression on Parker's face. "Can we please move on from this conversation? I don't think either one of you will win this particular battle."

"That is a smart woman you have on your arm tonight, Parker-poo. Don't fuck it up, okay?" Cami grinned as she took Maggs' hand and lead the way into the ballroom.

After getting dragged into a dance-off with Parker and Cami, I needed a break. Seeing I needed to be rescued, Brayden stole me away, and we explored what hors d'oeuvres there were and found a cocktail table to eat at.

"Are you having a good time?" Brayden asked, catching my hand and turning it over so he could trace a finger along my palm.

I nodded my head. "Yes, this has been a blast. Parker always seems to make things fun, even when I fail at it completely."

"Yes, he does have that habit..." he murmured, looking down at the table.

I grasped his hand, and he looked up at me. "I've missed you," I admitted. "I know we see each other every day and we spend time together, but it hasn't been just the two of us."

"Yeah, now that the others are stepping up their game, it's made catching you alone a little more challenging, but we'll figure it out. I need to be more intentional about asking you to do something with me, because it's going to be even harder once classes start up again," Brayden said, brushing his free hand along my cheek. "The only thing that helps is knowing that I'm connected to you and can reach to see how you're doing, even if I'm not there."

"That has taken some getting used to, learning whose feelings I'm feeling when, but now it's like comforting white noise in the background until I need it." I smiled. "I can't even imagine what it will be like when all five of you are rattling around in my head."

"Well, since I still have you to myself, would you care to

dance?" Brayden asked. His eyes sparkled with mirth and love as I let myself be led back to the ballroom.

This time the music changed, and it was more jazzy. This is when I'd been worried that they would be expecting us all to know how to jitterbug or foxtrot, but thankfully that wasn't the case. I spotted some people giving lessons on one part of the dance floor, but it wasn't what the majority of partygoers were doing. Brayden swept me into the flow of bodies and took over from there, which I was forever grateful for. Soon, I was able to get out of my own head—I'm sure the two glasses of champagne helped—and the next thing I knew, I was twirling into Hudson's arms. He pulled me close, and we swayed along to a smooth jazz song.

Bending down so his lips brushed my ear, he spoke loud enough so I could hear him. "I didn't get to tell you earlier, but you look ravishing, Sunshine."

"You don't look so bad yourself there, sir. Makes me want to have you leave it on the next time we're alone," I told him, nipping his earlobe, causing him to tighten his grip on my hip to drop lower to my ass.

"Whatever would please you, my Sunshine, I would be happy to do for you," Hudson purred, nuzzling into my neck.

Now that we had both turned each other on, which was very clear though our connection, we just clung to each other as we moved along the dance floor. All too soon, I was handed off to Jay for a much more formal waltz.

"Relax and let me lead," Jay instructed as I stumbled against his direction.

It was easier said than done, and I kept trying to figure out the steps so I would stop stumbling. Jay swung me wide then pulled me close so my back was to him, giving him the perfect moment to whisper in my ear. "Beautiful, you need to be a good girl and trust me to take the lead. I will not let anything happen to you, but you have to let go."

That right there, with the slight growl to his voice, made me melt as he pulled me away from him, back into the dance. This time, I closed my eyes and let him control my body, trusting he would keep me from crashing into anyone or doing anything else that might harm me. When I opened my eyes, there was a soft smile on Jay's lips that transformed his already handsome face into something that would make any woman drop her panties instantly. The hand that was on my shoulder slid around the back of my neck, and he applied pressure so I knew he was there but nothing that would alarm me. It was as if he flipped a switch, and when he pulled us into a dark corner, I was more than willing to meet his kiss as he pulled me up to him.

It wouldn't take much for someone to stumble upon us, but Jay's body mostly blocked me from sight. He started nipping down my neck, and I let it fall to the side so he had better access to it. A thumb swept over my nipple, causing me to gasp and clutch his biceps to keep my legs from giving out. This was the first time I could see the appeal of what it was that Jay loved about the possibility of being seen, the danger of getting caught. My whole body shivered, breaths coming out in shallow pants. I thought I might even come on the spot the more he teased me.

"Does my good girl need to come?" Jay asked, his lips whispering against my jaw.

I had to swallow before I could speak, my mouth having gone dry. "Yes…"

Jay placed his leg between mine and shifted my dress so my center was resting on it. "I can't do all the work, Beautiful. You're gonna need to help if you want to finish."

Shocked, I looked up at him, unsure of what he was talking about. Seeing my confusion, he took my hips and pulled them forward so I was rubbing along his thigh. I let out a cry of surprise, which he silenced with a kiss before he slid me back and forth until I got the rhythm and continued it on my own. He shifted his hand to my chest, letting his thumbs circle my hardened nipples, and when he felt me speeding up, on the edge of release, he pinched them both roughly. I collapsed against him, biting his shoulder to keep from crying out. Hugging me close, he ran a soothing hand up and down my back, whispering sweet words to me as I came down from my high. I never thought orgasms could get *more* intense, but that one was unlike anything else, and he didn't even have his dick in me.

Once I'd caught my breath, he righted my dress and led me back to the others, who all smirked and gave Jay a knowing look.

CHAPTER 24

LAILAH

Dancing, and my intimate moment with Jay, had landed us at thirty minutes till midnight, according to the announcement made through the hall. They asked everyone to come outside into the back courtyard that had champagne stations set up for everyone to get their glasses before the stroke of midnight. The whole courtyard was decorated and had performers wandering around as we waited, helping us to forget about the chilly bite in the night air. Parker took my hand and pulled me off to the side through a gate that led us to a small garden maze. Leading me through, he brought me to the center where there was a stone bench with a bottle of champagne set up and waiting for us.

"Did you plan this?" I asked Parker, clinging to his arm.

Parker grinned down at me and gave a playful wink. "Sure did, Trouble. I plan to keep you to myself just for a little while."

There were even blankets left so we could put one down on the bench and wrap the other around ourselves. "Parker, this is one of the most romantic things I think anyone has ever done for me."

"In a way, that makes me sad, but on the other hand, I'm

kinda glad that I got to be the first one to do it for you," Parker murmured as he placed a kiss on my temple.

"How will we know when the countdown happens if we're not with the rest of the party?" I asked when I noticed we couldn't really hear what was going on anymore.

Parker reached up and took my chin, turning my head to look at him. "Trust me, nothing else matters right now except for the two of us. Like you keep telling us, as long as we stick together, we'll be fine."

His words made me melt into a puddle of emotion. I never would have guessed that Parker had this side to him, knowing he was always drawn to being the comic relief, not taking life too seriously. Then again, he told me that he was going to be working on building the trust we had, and this moment was going a long way to that next level he was talking about.

Leaning into him, I let my head rest on his shoulder, enjoying the quiet moment we had under the stars. There wasn't even a cloud in the sky to cover them up. It was truly a magical moment, perfect to end one year and start another. All of a sudden, fireworks started shooting off all around us, splashing across the night in bright color, causing me to gasp. Surging to my feet, I slowly turned in a circle, taking it all in. Our party wasn't the only one shooting them off—there were several others too, making it seem as if the whole of Drittilyn was lit up by them.

When I turned back forward, I found Parker on one knee with his weapon in his hands, holding it up to me. "Lailah Mackenzie, I wish to give you my Oath as an Elementi Warrior."

My mouth dropped open, completely caught off guard. "What?"

"Lailah, bearer of Synergy, the sixth element, I would offer you my Oath if you will have it," Parker repeated, only this time I knew that the angelic aura was present to hear his plea.

"Parker, Knight blessed with Spirit's power, Warrior for the angels. I find you true of heart and mind, upholding the agreement given to your ancestors. Do you accept the eternal bond to protect the people of this world, and vow to cherish the vessel that holds the gift of Synergy, who has been placed in your protection?" I intoned.

"I, Parker Jones, Blessed Elementi Warrior gifted with Spirit's power, vow to cherish and protect this world, my fellow brothers, and the one bound to us as Synergy; or my life be forfeit," Parker answered, holding up his bladed staff to me.

"Rise, and seal your Oath," I said, reaching out my hand for him.

Parker grasped it and stood, pulling me to his chest, but before I could kiss him, he stopped me. "I want you to know that I am giving you my Oath right now but not my Bond. There is still more that I have to prove to you before I can allow you to accept me for the rest of eternity. In giving you my Oath, I have announced to you and the heavens above that I am in this to the bitter end. No matter what happens with the others, or how they might dislike me, or think I'm not good enough to be an Elementi Warrior, I will not give up on you or them."

I didn't even realize that I was crying until he wiped away my tears with his thumbs. "Thank you, Parker."

Leaning down, he kissed me. It wasn't the normal, heated kiss that led to blind passion right after the Oath was given. This sent a surge through my heart and forged a new and budding connection to him and his powers. I didn't have the small ball of energy sharing space with the others, but there was a faint purple line showing our blossoming Bond. We indulged in the sweet moment, sitting curled up on the bench, drinking champagne and sharing lingering kisses that warmed my very soul. All too soon it was time for us to head back to the others, but this was one New Year's Eve I was never going to forget.

When we returned to the party to search for the others, a woman let out a blood-curdling scream. Everyone burst into action, and if Parker hadn't grabbed me close to his chest, I would have been swept away from the people running out of the wing where the dancing was. Looking up at Parker and catching his gaze, he nodded his head, and taking a firm hold on my hand, we headed against the flow. Having a tall, solid man as a shield while you had hundreds of people running was invaluable. Finally, we made our way into the room and easily found what caused everyone to panic.

On the stage where the band was playing, everything had been shoved off so all that was left was the dead woman bleeding out. The other four guys were by the stage. Micah was on the phone with someone, and Jay was taking pictures of the scene. When Brayden saw us enter the room, he shook his head no, and Parker halted.

"Why are you stopping? We need to see what's going on," I demanded.

Parker looked from me back to the stage and shook his head. "If Brayden says not to let you go over there, then I'm gonna do what he says. I trust that he is always thinking of you first, even if you're not gonna like it."

He wasn't wrong about that, but if I was going to be a part of this team, then I needed to know what was going on.

"Look, I'm sorry, but I don't need to be so protected that I can't be of help, Parker," I snapped, jerking my arm out of his hold and taking off towards the stage.

The others were too distracted dealing with the scene, not noticing me until I was right by them and was able to see what they'd been trying to keep from me.

YOU CAN'T SAVE THEM ALL, BUT YOU CAN STOP IT... THEIR BLOOD IS ON YOUR HANDS.

Unable to hold it back, I let out a mournful, wailing sob, crumpling to the ground where I proceeded to retch up everything I'd eaten that night. Brayden swore and grabbed me around the waist, hauling me away from the scene. The woman was sprawled out naked on the stage with a symbol carved into her stomach and her throat slashed. Ubel—because there was no doubt in my mind it was him—had used her blood to write the note, and it made me sick knowing he was just getting started. He didn't get his first victim since I saved that little boy, so he had to try again.

So much for my magical New Year.

I went back to the house with Brayden and Parker while the others stayed back to work with the Elementi and their police connections. The whole ride back I couldn't stop shaking, but I'd managed to stop crying. Brayden wouldn't set me down yet, so I was carried up the stairs to our wing.

"I'm so sorry, Angel," Brayden whispered in my ear as he set me down. "This man is a sick bastard, but we are going to do everything we can to get his ass."

Letting out a shaky breath, I looked up at him. "I should have trusted you when you told Parker not to let me see what was going on. I'm sorry I didn't listen. That poor woman's family... she's dead because of me."

"No, I'm not letting you go down that road, Lailah. What this man chooses to do does not fall on your shoulders. He is fucked up in the head and was already evil enough that the Dark Lord didn't need to make him a host. That alone should tell you the special kind of crazy he is," Parker growled, scrunching up in anger. "What we need to be prepared for now is that anything can happen anywhere."

"There is nothing we can do right now that isn't already happening. Go get ready for bed and come find one of us. We'll stay with you," Brayden reassured.

Still shaking slightly, I decided a shower would be the best thing, needing to wash this night from my body. Once changed into my pajamas, I wandered into Parker's room where he sat on the bed, shirtless in grey sweatpants. A surge of heat flooded my body at the sight of him, the urge to Bond uncaring that I'd gone through a traumatic event tonight. One look at my face, and Parker swept me up into a tight hug.

"I think it would be best for you not to sleep here tonight, Trouble. The draw to seal the Bond will only grow stronger if we are so close," Parker said, kissing the top of my head. "I know this is terrible timing to say something, but I was kind of hoping that you might keep what happened between us tonight quiet for now. I didn't do it for them. I needed to make sure you knew how serious I am about you. I feel like the others won't get it."

Looking up at him, I searched his eyes. "Okay, I guess I get that, but I don't think they'll react the way you think they will."

"Trouble, I love that you always see the best in people, but at this moment they don't trust me with you alone farther than they can throw me. I just don't want to add more fuel to the flames already nipping at my heels. Once things have mellowed out, then I will happily tell them myself, but let's deal with one problem at a time." Parker sighed, running his fingers through my hair as I leaned on his chest.

"Fine, but if they ask me, I'm not going to lie to them," I countered.

"I would never ask you to lie, Trouble. That would make me the biggest asshole known to man, and Micah has held that role for a long time. I wouldn't want to knock him down from his throne."

Smiling, I pulled away and gave him a quick kiss. "Alright, I'll see you in the morning."

"Night, Trouble. Sweet dreams," Parker said with a soft smile.

I let out a harsh laugh as I shut Parker's door. "Yeah I'm not sure sweet dreams are going to happen, but there's always hope, I guess."

I headed over to Brayden's room, finding him already in bed reading as he waited for me. Seeing me, he didn't say a word but lifted the comforter for me as I crawled in, wrapping myself around him. I could feel how worried he was about me, even if he didn't say it. Hell, I was worried about me too, but there was nothing we could do to fix it at the moment.

CHAPTER 25
MICAH

The rage that filled my soul at the sight of what this evil son of a bitch had done was like nothing I had ever felt before. Add in the fact that he was doing this to the woman I was pretty sure I was in love with, and it brought this to a whole other level. After ignoring us, Parker, the fuckwit, let her see this horrific sight, and it sent her into shock—crying and shaking, unable to talk. I knew that Lailah asked me to try, but that idiot just kept screwing up time after time, and I couldn't stand it.

If he wanted to dick around with any other girl, that would be fine, but not this one—never this one. Lailah was everything good and pure, and someone like me had no business even thinking I had a chance with her. It was one reason I fought so hard against her, but now it was becoming clear what an utter ass I'd been about the whole thing.

"What do we know?" Jay asked, pulling me out of my thoughts and back to the matter at hand.

When we discovered what happened, Jay got on the phone with the Elementi right away, trying to make sure we intercepted the police. There was an unwritten rule with law enforcement of all branches that if we claimed something, we would be allowed to handle it first and then pass it off to the appropriate people to deal with once we were done. This murder would have gotten the attention of some of the bigger human intelligence branches, and we didn't want to go ten rounds with them right now on who would take over.

"The only time he would have had to do this was during the countdown and the fireworks after," Hudson answered, making notes on his phone. "The display lasted ten minutes, so he roughly had twenty by the time everyone left the room when it all started. That isn't much time..."

"How could he have done all of this so quickly?" I wondered. "There is too much blood for this to have happened elsewhere."

Jay started to look around the room, searching for something, then headed off to the left of the space. We followed him as he found a back door that had an alarm that would sound if you opened it without the key. Before we could stop him, he thrust the door open, and nothing happened.

"Son of a bitch must have cut the alarm off," I snarled. "Hell, he could have changed himself to look like one of the staff."

Walking out behind the event building, we found dumpsters and an open area for the band to unload their trailer. Using our phones for flashlights, we searched the space for any other clues.

"Guys..." Jay called. "I found who he pretended to be, or else it was someone who got in his way."

Off in a dark corner, near a brick wall hiding this area from guests' eyes, was a man crumpled in the corner with his throat slashed. Jay squatted down and took a picture of the man's face. "Now at least we can figure out who this guy was and if he worked here or not. If he's just another guest, that doesn't help us much."

I watched Hudson flinch at Jay's unemotional remark, but I understood what he was trying to say. When you're chasing after a ghost who could be anyone, you needed all the information you could get. Heading back inside, I walked over to the team leader of the Elementi unit that showed up.

Looking at the man's uniform, I saw the last name "Johansson" written on it. "There's another dead body out back. Looks like another victim of our friend here," I said, motioning to the back door.

Johansson nodded his head and grabbed his radio. "Blake, we need another body bag and removal from the back of the building. We'll need to bring this one back to HQ as well."

"Roger that."

"Hey, you're one of the Knights, right? Can I ask you something?" Johansson asked.

"You can ask, doesn't mean I'll answer," I quipped, shrugging my shoulders.

Johansson blinked at me a moment, probably not expecting that type of answer, but it was one in the morning and I didn't have a fuck to give.

"Did you know there was a chance someone might be killed tonight?" Johansson questioned. "Is that why you were at this party? Just doesn't seem like the scene a kid like yourself would want to hang out at."

"No, one of the others wanted to take our girlfriend, and the rest of us didn't want to spend the night without her, so we came," I snarked. "Oh, and just so we're clear, you have no idea what kind of scene you would find me at, and I'm no kid. The shit I've seen would make you piss yourself. It causes you to lose what innocence you have when the demon behind the curtain is a real thing to you," I answered bluntly.

"Micah," Hudson called. "Leave the man alone. We're leaving."

I turned to walk away, but Johansson grabbed my arm. "Listen here, you little shit, I fought in wars to keep this country safe before you were even born. Don't look down on others who are able to give you a safe world to live in."

The small thread holding my anger in check snapped. I grabbed the man's wrist and squeezed the joint, knowing if I kept going, I could break it easily. "I hate to tell you this, but you've got it all wrong. I'm the one who is keeping the world safe from the demons and their master who wants to destroy it just because they can. So, when you lay there in your bed tonight thinking of the woman dead on the stage, just know that the only thing standing between you and the demon who did it is a team of six so-called *kids*." Tossing off his hold, I shoved past him, smirking as I heard him swear.

"Was that necessary?" Hudson sighed.

"Nope, but it sure felt good." I grinned, clapping him on the back as we exited the event hall. "What'd I miss?"

Jay, who was already outside, handed me his phone, showing me a picture of a series of symbols burnt into the asphalt. Since Mr. Creed and I got along so well, he'd decided to teach me far more than any of the others since he could stand to spend time with me. Thanks to that extra education, I could pick out more than half of these and groan at their meaning. "This fucker is good, I'll give him that. He was able to create an illusion of some kind and a circle of silence, which is why he got away with it in such a public place."

"So we need to start thinking of this man as more of a demonic warlock instead of a simple-minded demon," Hudson theorized.

A harsh laugh burst out of me at his thought. "Yeah, this guy is anything but the average demon wanting to cause the usual kind of trouble."

"I already sent them to Creed. He said he'll be ready to give us a briefing on what he knows about Ubel and the symbols I sent him from the pond," Jay interjected.

"Fuck, Lailah is gonna be pissed when she finds out we haven't told her everything," I grumbled. None of us wanted to ruin this night for her, but this asshole did it anyway.

"We'll deal with that once we've gotten some sleep and we make sure telling her won't send her into another spiral," Hudson said as we got into the car Beth sent over for us.

"No." Jay stated. "We need to tell her, no matter what. Others might keep secrets from their woman, but *we* will NOT."

There was something in his tone that told me this was way more of a personal issue than it was about us not telling Lailah things, but I had to agree with him. Nothing good ever came from keeping secrets, and the Elementi Warriors would always be asked to live up to a higher standard, following the creed the angels gave to the first five men all those centuries ago.

"Jay's right. We tell her everything we know, then we teach her how to deal with it like they've taught all of us. Cookie Monster's winter vacation is officially over, and Elementi boot camp is now in session." I heaved a heavy sigh. "Get ready for the backlash, boys. It's not gonna be pretty."

CHAPTER 26

LAILAH

"What do you mean Ubel can change his appearance?!" I blurted, pausing with my tea halfway to my mouth.

It was a fitful night's sleep for me and the others, so we all ended up coming down for breakfast super early. Thankfully, Sarah and Garrett were already up and working on prepping breakfast, so we all got out of their hair with coffee and tea.

"We will explain that part better once Mr. Creed shows up and fills us in on that and the symbols that Jay found back at the lake and at the event hall," Micah continued.

Setting my mug down, I glared at all the guys. "Why am I just finding out about this now? This information is kind of a big deal, don't you think?"

"None of us wanted to stress you out or ruin New Year's Eve for you when we didn't have all the information yet. I agree that it wasn't the best choice for us to make, but we are telling you now. Everything is out on the table, so to speak. No more secrets or held back information from this moment forward," Hudson said, rubbing his hand soothingly up and down my back.

I knew he could feel how hurt I felt at them once again acting like I wasn't truly part of this team. Just when I thought we had gotten past that, it seemed their need to be overprotective was stronger than their ability to tell me things that might upset me. Both Hudson and Brayden felt guilty for not telling me, and their regret rippled over my skin. I got the feeling this time they realized what withholding information did to me.

"In the effort of keeping you in the loop, your training starts today," Jay added as he calmly drank from his cup, watching my reaction with his dark gray eyes.

As if Tony was listening in to our conversation, he texted me to ask if we could move the assessment up to today in light of everything going on.

"You flirting with someone there, Trouble?" Parker asked, trying to peer over my shoulder at my phone as he walked by to get more coffee.

Rolling my eyes, I looked up at him. "You really think I have time for another guy when I have the five of you to deal with? Not a chance. It was just Tony telling me we're meeting for my assessment later today."

"That's right, I forgot you knew Tony. He totally cockblocked me that first day we met." Parker frowned as he sat back down.

"So, we have a meeting with Mr. Creed and I'm doing training with Tony—anything else you guys planned that I need to know about?" I inquired.

Brayden just smirked and shook his head with a little chuckle. "Nona wanted to check in on you and go over a few things before starting with her tomorrow. Other than that, I think that's all. Beth was the one who was heading that up once we updated her on our findings last night."

"Great. Now I have to have this same conversation with Beth about leaving me in the dark about things that you know involve me. Don't you think it's a little odd that you know all this before I do? I mean, Brayden, you were with me all night. How did you find out?" I grumbled.

"Easy there, Angel, put the claws away. Check your email, because that's where I got my information from this morning," Brayden said, holding up his hands in defense.

Sure enough, when I looked at my email, she had sent over an updated schedule for me and the guys. Everything was tailored to deal with the issues we were now facing. This is what I needed; I didn't do well when I felt so uninformed. Having something to focus on when everything else around me was going crazy helped me deal with my stress when I didn't have the ability to run.

Speaking of stress, I noticed that Micah was hardly able to sit at the table with us, his leg bouncing as he glowered down at his black coffee. He still hadn't actually spoken yet, but I did notice that when Parker joined us, his frown was even deeper than before. Fingers crossed Tony could come up with a way to help us.

I'd been down to the lower level where the Elementi set up their headquarters under the Manor, but I hadn't seen all that much of it. I knew that it was quite expansive, having tunnels and other facilities under the whole of Ryevick University. I followed after the boys since they knew where they were going, and I scoped out the place. All the hallways were white tile with soft gray walls and lots of bright lighting overhead. Each of the main sections, I was told, was named after an element so it was easier to learn the layout. We were in the Earth section, so all the pictures depicted that information along with green doors. Everything here had biometric scanners to open doors and access computers and the like. I felt like I was in some James Bond movie rather than an elite underground society.

Finally, we entered what looked like a small library with lots of haunting art hanging from the walls. A large black desk was off to one side, and it dawned on me that this must be Mr. Creed's workspace. Taking a closer look at the books, I found they were all about the occult and anything else that might tie back to demons and their history.

"Ah, good. Right on time," Mr. Creed said as he hurried into the room, plopping various books and scrolls on his desk.

The man was portly with greasy, slicked-back hair—or what was left of it—and a piggish face. He seemed to always wear suits that didn't fit him around the middle, his button holding his jacket closed by sheer willpower alone.

"Don't just stand there gawking at me, sit down. We have lots to cover, so don't interrupt me until I've finished speaking. Then we can go over whatever questions you might have," Mr. Creed said, looking right at Parker with a slight frown.

Heading over to the small seating area, we managed to squeeze onto the couch and two armchairs. To make extra room, Micah snaked his arm around my waist and pulled me onto his lap. I looked back at him, opening my mouth to yell, but he just put a finger up to my lips, shushing me.

"Let's start with what we do know and then deal with the uncertain bits later," Mr. Creed suggested as he walked over to one of the bookshelves and pulled down a projector screen. Using the clicker he had in his hand, he displayed a picture of a creepy looking man with a wheel of heads, both male and female. "This is Dantalion, the seventy-first of Solomon's demons. Among the many names he's been given over the centuries, the Great Duke of Hell, master of a legion of thirty-six demons. He is also referred to as The Man with Many Faces since he has been depicted with different faces or genders throughout history. He is the keeper of the Forbidden Library, where all demonic alliances and secrets are kept."

Flipping to the next slide, it showed a symbol surrounded by other smaller ones etched into the dirt. "This is his summoning mark, and it was found at the pond where this Ubel surfaced.

Scouring through all of my books, I came to find that Ubel is the name of one of the thirty-six demons that Dantalion has command over. Could it be pure coincidence that he picked that name? No, I think not. With the other findings, it seems as if the Duke of Hell has given this man access to his powers on the command of the Dark Lord."

The next slide pulled up a clearer version of the smaller markings. "These are powerful symbols to invoke; they require skill and raw power. Only a higher-level demon or one of the seventy-two Greater Demons that make up the Dark Lord's court could pull this off. Which leads me to believe that the Dark Lord has awoken them and is preparing to use those unlocked humans that are given the demonic serum to host their powers to unleash on the world."

My jaw fell open at this dramatic turn of events and how utterly serious he was in his findings. It wasn't that I didn't believe him—I, of all people, knew how the Dark Lord loved to play games—but this version didn't sit right with me.

Parker raised his hand, causing Mr. Creed to sigh. "Yes, Mr. Jones?"

"I'm just trying to figure out how we went from one of the lowest of the Greater Demons being awoken to having them all awake and terrorizing the world..." Parker asked, scratching his jaw as he squinted at the screen.

Mr. Creed scowled at him. "Did you not hear a word I just said?"

"No, I got all that, but these smaller symbols don't show any clues to more of the Greater Demons waking up. On that note, what do we know about the Dark Lord? Is he really the ruler of Hell, or is that just another title like the Grand Duke of Hell? He might not be able to wake up the stronger of the greater demons," Parker asked, starting to ramble as he thought out loud.

"Enough," Mr. Creed snapped. "We are losing sight of what's really at stake here."

Hudson shifted so his elbows rested on his knees, looking at Mr. Creed. "I don't think so. Parker has made a few good points. From what we know, there are demons of all kinds, ranks, and species, but never once have we been told who the true ruler of Hell is, with seven princes claiming that job."

"This is what you want to debate now, Mr. Lacy, while there is a serial killer on the loose?"

"Once again, I believe you are taking this in the wrong direction. Yes, we need to understand Ubel and what he's trying to do, but that doesn't mean all of Hell is behind this. The Dark Lord could also be part of the Greater Demons of Solomon or one of the Seven Princes of Hell, we just don't know because he's using another name. If all the Seven Princes of Hell decided to wipe out the Earth, then I don't think the Elementi could stop them," Hudson challenged.

Slowly, I raised my hand, knowing that I might be fanning the flames with this question. "Ah, sorry, new to all this, but how do we know the Greater Demons are all asleep?"

"Many people try to summon them, but you have to have enough power to pull them out of Hell. Those of weaker power are not as affected by leaving Hell, but these are. They need demonic power to live off of, and there isn't enough here for them. Think of it this way, the higher the rank the more demonic power they need. The Seven Princes of Hell are at the top, then the Greater Demons, higher-level, mid-level, then lower demons. So, to Mr. Creed's point, by having these people changed by the demonic serum, they will become hosts and provide more demonic energy on Earth for them to live off of," Micah explained. "So way back in BC times, when Solomon called his legion of seventy-two Greater Demons and enslaved them to build the temple, they became too weak to leave Hell once they returned. As far as we know, they have been in slumber ever since—or at least, that's what we are led to believe from what we've been able to pull out of the lower demons. No one truly knows what goes on in Hell, and we have to go by what the angels have provided for us and knowledge we have gathered over the years."

Mr. Creed took a book off his desk and brought it over to me, holding it out. "This book contains all the names of those seventy-two Greater Demons and their abilities, along with the other basic types of demons. This is where we will be starting your education that has been ignored for far too long."

"Would it be worth asking the Dark Lord who he is?" I asked, looking at everyone.

"What?!" Mr. Creed gasped. "Why on earth would you do such a thing? Knowing a demon's true name is to gain power over them. It is the one thing you need to know in order to summon them here."

"Even if he doesn't answer, I'm sure I will get more information out of him. He loves to taunt me with all I don't know," I pushed, needing to find something good out of this special attention the Dark Lord kept showering on me.

Mr. Creed harrumphed at my comment. "If you weren't as ignorant as a baby deer then I might ponder the idea, but there is no way I would let *you* deal with something so sensitive."

Micah tensed, hugging me tightly. "Watch it, Creed. I like you, but I won't let you talk to her that way."

The two were locked in a battle of wills, eyes narrowed at each other before Mr. Creed turned away first. "Fine. Let her do what she wants, but if she ends up killing herself or getting tied to a Greater Demon, then that is on you lot."

"Perhaps it would be better if we went back to the symbols? We found more last night. I know Micah figured a good majority of them out, but is there anything we missed?" Hudson redirected.

"Yes, as a matter of fact, there was something on the body

you all missed. Carved into her back was another symbol, and this one was to feed the energy of this sacrifice to another. I didn't recognize the marking, so it could very well be this Dark Lord of ours, but it still lets us know that there is a more powerful demon here that needs the demonic energy to survive. If they can't get it directly from Hell, then it seems they're going to make it here with spells until they can distribute the serum," Mr. Creed announced.

"Fuck—this just got a whole hell of a lot worse," Parker muttered.

"I couldn't agree more," Mr. Creed said with a nod of his head.

CHAPTER 27

LAILAH

Mr. Creed went over a few more things with us and gave me two more books to start looking over before we left his study. Now I needed to go back to my room and change to meet with Tony for my assessment down in the humongous gym. There was a full weight room, a boxing ring, basketball court, and even an indoor track.

"Why didn't anyone tell me there was an INDOOR TRACK??" I demanded when I caught sight of it, turning to glare at the guys.

"Ah..." Parker said, rubbing the back of his neck. "Yeah, sorry Trouble, I totally forgot we had that down here."

Jay walked up to me and pulled me against his chest with a little smirk on his lips. "I didn't tell you because I like having alone time with you. If we run here, they'll turn up." He motioned with his head.

"Okay, that's kind of really sweet, but it's been two months since I've been able to run outside! Why didn't you tell me then?" I countered, trying to still be irritated with him but failing.

Jay shrugged his shoulders and looked at the track. "I hate running underground."

"The gang's all here. Hmm, I don't remember telling you guys to come for an assessment?" Tony smirked as he entered the gym with Cami right behind him.

Tony was a large, buff black man with warm brown eyes. His thick black hair was cut to the skin on the side and left about an inch on top. Today, he looked much more relaxed in his basketball shorts and t-shirt, versus his security uniform.

"I believe you owe me twenty bucks, big man." Cami grinned, holding out her hand.

Returning her grin, he slapped her hand and kept walking. "I never said I agreed to the bet, short stop. I try not to lose money to you unnecessarily."

"What the hell are you doing here, ankle biter?" Micah asked, arms crossed.

"Did you forget so soon, flame boy? We have a match to settle things between us, or are you too scared to lose?" Cami taunted.

"Oh, it's on, bite-size. Prepare to get your ass burnt," Micah tossed back.

I couldn't help it. I burst out laughing as they tossed insults back and forth, standing toe to toe, with Cami's hands on her hips, glaring up at him. The size difference between them made it that much more funny.

"Easy now, you two. We're going to deal with that a bit later, when I'm done with Lailah. I'm glad you're all here—I thought it might be fun to start the new year with a little tournament, test your skills and see what needs work," Tony interjected, pulling Cami away by the back of her shirt. "Now, you guys entertain yourself until I get this assessment done."

The group split off to do their own workouts, leaving me with Tony.

"Alright, now Cami tells me you were on the track team. Did

they have you working with free weights or just drills on the track field?" Tony asked me, looking over his clipboard.

"Typically, we did a lot of drills on the field, but when it was winter we worked out more in the gym. Hard to run in snow and ice."

Tony nodded his head and stopped at the edge of the stretching floor. "Let's warm up and see what your flexibility is like. Kill two birds with one stone. First, I have to ask—are you okay with me assisting you and adjusting your form?"

"Yup, not a problem," I answered, waving off the question. "I'd rather you help me fix something that I've done wrong before I hurt myself than freak out over an assist."

"I hear ya, but I want to make sure you are totally comfortable, and I don't need five pissed off dudes with magic powers coming after me." He laughed. "Alright, follow my lead."

It was nice to be back in the gym and working out, and I really needed the stretching after all the crazy of the last few days. Then, once I was warmed up, we headed to the weights and worked out my whole body. We didn't push it too far, just tested to see when I reached my limit. Finally, we got to the best part—Tony wanted to see how fast I could run.

"Look, I know you've been off a few months and haven't really been training, so don't go crazy. I just want a gauge of where your stamina is. We're going for distance, not just speed, although I would be lying if I didn't tell you I was going to time your 200 meter dash," Tony said as he pulled out his stopwatch.

I lined up and got into position on the starting block, my body all too willing to fall right back into the swing of things. The sound of a buzzer signaled the start of the race, and I took off down the track. I felt myself let everything fade away as I focused on the goal at hand, the sound of my feet on the ground accented by the beating of my heart all I could hear. This was my safe place, the one thing I could do to let the world fall away and just be. I didn't worry about time or how long I was going to run. I just let my body's instincts take over, trusting it to know just how far I could push myself. Finally, when my legs started to burn and my breath was sawing out of my lungs, I started to slow down and did another lap at a more leisurely pace so I didn't cramp up the moment I stopped.

"Holy shit Lala, that was crazy!" Cami exclaimed when I returned to the starting point where everyone was waiting. "What distance was that, even?"

Tony looked down at his clipboard, adding something up before he looked at me wide-eyed. "You just ran a 10k in a little under an hour without any prior training. Woman, what were you like on your track team?"

"Oh, well that time would be a little slow for me when I was competing. I typically could do that in forty-five minutes, sometimes a little less. Before you guys get really impressed, the Olympic level is like thirty minutes, okay," I said blushing.

"Well, I surely don't need to worry about you being able to run away fast enough if something bad goes down," Tony said with a smile. "Now, go stretch out while I get this little tournament figured out with these idiots."

Nodding, I headed over to the side and flopped to the ground to start my cooldown. When I sat up from a stretch, a water bottle was hanging in the air by my face. Grabbing it, I looked around and saw Jay with a smirk on his face. Had he just used his air powers to send me over a bottle of water? Then he winked. Yup, that confirmed it—Jay was showing off, and I quite enjoyed it. Confident that I wouldn't cramp up from my workout and the run, I headed back over to the group, heading right to Jay.

I bumped him with my hip, causing him to look at me. "Thanks for the water."

"I noticed you forgot to bring one, and it isn't smart to let yourself get dehydrated," Jay mentioned, cocking a scolding eyebrow at me.

This made me smile even more. "Thankfully, I have a very attentive boyfriend to make sure I'm well looked after."

A cough sounded, pulling my attention back to the others, who were watching the two of us with amused looks.

"If you two are done flirting, we have a tournament to start," Tony admonished.

Feeling my cheeks heat with embarrassment, I looked down at my feet. "Sorry."

Jay slipped his hand into mine and gave it a squeeze but didn't let go; instead, he threaded his fingers through mine.

"Alright, we're going to start with Micah and Cami. The rules for you two are simple: no powers and no nut shots. The first one to get their opponent to tap out wins. Oh, and try not to kill each other, alright?" Tony instructed, holding the ropes apart for the two of them to enter into the boxing ring.

Cami and Micah already had their hands wrapped and were wearing knuckle gloves. Micah bounced on the balls of his feet, shaking out his arms as he waited while Cami did some last-minute stretches.

"Fighters meet," Tony called, and they came to the center. "Fighters ready... and fight!"

Micah started out swinging, but Cami ducked low and elbowed him in the gut.

"Not off to such a good start there," Cami taunted as they broke apart, beginning to circle each other, watching and waiting for the next move.

Cami charged at Micah and he braced himself for a hit, but she leapt at him like a puma taking down its prey. She wrapped her legs around his waist and took him down to the mats with a resounding *THUD*. Cami started to wail on Micah, hitting him where she could reach, but Micah was able to shield himself for the most part.

"What the fuck is this?! You're fighting like some angry drunk chick at a bar," Micah spat as he tried to hold his own.

"This is how you're going to prove to me that you can keep Lailah safe?"

Having had enough, Micah kicked his legs up and was able to trap her around her neck, pulling his legs down and bending her backwards while he rolled, dislodging her. He swept her away, giving himself time to stand and prepare for the next attack.

They came together in a flurry of kicks, blocks, and punches so fast it was hard to tell what landed and what didn't. Then Micah took Cami down to the mats, but that didn't mean the fight was over. Cami refused to allow Micah to take whatever hold he was trying to, squirming around like an eel. Then, somehow, they both ended up in this impossible knot of limbs neither one of them could get out of.

A whistle blast sounded, and both Micah and Cami released each other. "That's a tie!" Tony called.

Micah helped Cami to stand.

"Guess we'll have to try again next year," Micah grumbled.

Frowning, I looked at them both. "Wait, you've done this before?"

"Hell yeah girl, we have a rematch every year!" Cami explained as she hopped out of the ring.

"Why do I feel like you guys totally played me on this?" I asked, and I couldn't help but pout just a little.

Cami hugged me around my waist so her head was resting on my chest. "Don't be like that, Lala. It helps us get past the shit that builds up between us, otherwise one of us would explode on the other."

"Cami, get your face out of my girlfriend's boobs. That's a low blow, even for you," Micah growled, stalking over to her.

Cami dropped her arms and backed away slowly before sticking her tongue out at him. "You're just jealous because I'm the perfect height to use them as pillows when I hug her."

Micah swept me up, wrapping my legs around his waist with

his hand holding my ass and kissed the hell out of me. I let out a little squeak before I melted into him and curled my fingers into his hair that was pulled up.

"Okay, okay, you two, no making out while there's an instructor present," Tony grumbled.

"I take it you're still single, Tony?" Micah asked as he let me down.

Tony gave him a look that would have made a weaker man flinch. "You still a dick?"

Micah chuckled and shrugged his shoulders in answer.

"Now, for the rest of you lot, we'll need to go into one of the warded training rooms so we don't have your powers bringing this place down around our ears," Tony said, waving for us to follow him. "Cami, I think it's best if we keep this a closed event, hit the showers and I'll see you tomorrow for training."

Down another hall in the Water section, there were six steel doors with warning lights on the outside to show if the room was in use or not. Tony took us to the last one and opened the door for us to enter. When I stepped inside, I could feel the hum of an electric current running along my skin, raising the hair on the back of my neck. The room itself was lined with black steel paneling on the walls with different symbols and phrases written on them in white. When I brushed my fingers over one of them, I felt a zap like I'd gotten a static shock.

"This whole room is covered in wards to stop our powers from leaking outside. It takes a little to get used to it, but soon you won't even notice the energy dampeners," Hudson shared as he stood next to me. "This is our team training room; the others are for single use and are much smaller."

Taking in the rest of the room, I noticed a white circle drawn on the floor that a circus could use for its performances. It made sense, though, that this was larger, since the five of them needed to work on things together—well, now six of us. It did make me feel much better knowing that I would be able to safely practice my powers with Nona and not have to worry about things getting crazy.

"In the interest of being fair, I picked the pairings for the first round: Micah and Parker, Jay and Lailah, Hudson and Brayden," Tony announced.

"What?!" Micah snapped. "Lailah isn't doing this; she doesn't even know how to fight!"

Tony just rolled his eyes at Micah. "That is why I have her with Jay. I want to see what her instinctual reactions to things are. Her powers will protect her if she trusts them to do so."

Micah muttered under his breath, but he let the issue go.

"Lailah, why don't you and Jay go first so that we can get it over with and everyone can calm down," Tony suggested, motioning to the ring.

Taking a deep, calming breath, I stepped into the circle, and Jay joined me. When we were both inside, he said some complicated phrase that sounded like Latin, and the hum in the room got louder as the white outline glowed and then settled once more.

"I activated the ring so we can't harm anyone outside of this circle," Jay mentioned as he stood in the middle. "The plan is that I will use simple attacks on you to see how your power responds on its own. All you need to do is trust that it will keep you safe and give into what your gut tells you to do."

Nodding, I took a moment to center myself and let my power flow through my body, ready and waiting for me to use it. Jay took a step back, gathering a swirling ball of wind in his hand, and hurled it at me. Instantly, I had my sai in my hands crossed in front of me, blocking his attack while the wind buffeted against me.

I could feel my feet slipping on the concrete floor as the wind pushed against me. I needed to dispel it before it would dissipate. My power flowed down my arms and seeped into the sai, causing them to glow and pulse a bright shade of gold, causing the attack to poof out of existence. Then Jay was there in my space wrapping me up in a tornado of sorts, but my power wrapped me up in a golden bubble and pushed out against the wind until it once again caused it to dissipate.

Time and time again, Jay attacked, and I muddled my way through getting out of each situation, but the common theme was I could shield against them and my powers could break apart his spell once it touched my shield.

"Okay, Lailah, now try and attack Jay. Even if it's just to push him away when he gets too close," Tony called out.

I was panting, and sweat soaked through my shirt with the amount of power I'd been using. I wasn't even sure I'd be able to put that much strength behind an attack. Jay, true to who he was, didn't give me a chance to doubt myself and charged at me.

I was terrified to hurt him, and my tank was running on empty.

So what did my power do?

It decided to pull from Jay, causing him to crash into me, knocking us to the floor, when I couldn't move out of the way fast enough. His energy surged into me, and I could feel him panic ever so slightly, but it was enough that I felt him taking the last of what power I had left, trying to compensate for what I was taking from him. This turned us into an endless cycle of power flowing between the two of us until it seemed that my golden power mixed into his silver, creating this beautiful energy between us.

His lips found mine, and I couldn't resist him, letting his hand grab onto my hair and pull my head back so he could deepen the kiss. My arms and legs wrapped around him until I was practically fused to him from lips to groin. Power pulsed between us as a pure white light surrounded us and a voice echoed through the air, causing us to break apart.

"Jalen Minh, Knight blessed with Air's power, Warrior for the angels, we accept your Oath and find you true and worthy."

CHAPTER 28

LAILAH

When we both came back to our senses and the white light was gone, I was still wrapped around Jay, but this time we were sitting instead of laying down. Looking around, I found the guys yelling at each other and making gestures towards the barrier that was keeping them out. It also dawned on me that I couldn't hear them. Had something changed? Moments ago, Tony had been able to talk to me, so why couldn't I hear now? Jay, still holding me, stood and said another intricate phrase, dropping the wards on the circle. They guys rushed in and surrounded us, all speaking at once.

"What the actual fuck just happened?"

"Angel, are you okay?"

"What was that bright light? How did it change the barrier so we couldn't get to you?"

"God damn it, Trouble, don't scare us like that! So not cool."

Still a little shocked and disoriented, I clung to Jay, hiding my face in his neck. The energy between us thrummed through my body, telling me that what just happened wasn't a dream. Somehow, without having to utter a word, Jay had given me his Oath and the angels had accepted it. Why was I shocked?

Honestly, I don't know, because Jay was always actions over words.

"Guys, enough," Jay said, silencing them all instantly. "She's fine. It was my fault. I didn't think it would happen like this, but it did—Lailah accepted my Oath."

"Wait, what? You didn't say anything though?" Parker challenged.

Micah turned on Parker and slammed him into the wall with his hand around Parker's throat. "How would you know that? You weren't around when any of the others gave their Oaths."

"Let me go," Parker gasped while Tony tried to break them up.

"Not until you give me an answer, you cock sucker," Micah seethed.

Parker reached up and grabbed Micah's wrist with both his hands and launched himself at him. They rolled on the ground, swearing, kicking, and punching until they were back in the circle. The rest of us had moved out of it, so when one of them said the incantation, sending the barrier walls back up, it was just the two of them. Micah shoved Parker away as he hopped up to his feet, his dual swords ready in his hands. Parker followed suit with his long-bladed staff, wiping the blood off his face from getting hit in the nose.

"What gives you the right to even ask me that question? You had the chance to be with her and you turned it the fuck down. So what if I gave her my Oath and she accepted it? That is between the two of us, not the rest of you," Parker growled.

Micah let out a battle cry filled with rage and descended upon Parker, blades and bodies moving so fast I couldn't keep up with what was going on. Still in Jay's hold, I turned to him. "Can they truly hurt each other in there?"

Jay looked at me a moment, and I could see him weighing the answer before he spoke. "Yes, they can hurt each other, or even kill one another."

"Why isn't anyone stopping them?!" I gasped, trying to wriggle out of Jay's hold.

Jay leaned down and bit my earlobe. "Be still, Beautiful. This needs to happen if there is any hope of the two of them mending things. There is lots of pent-up anger that goes beyond you."

As much as I hated it, I knew deep down he was right. After all, this had been my whole plan to get them to work things out. I just didn't understand how volatile it would be when it happened. All I could do now was wait and watch for two men that I loved and cared deeply about to figure their issues out their own way. Bursts of flame flashed as Micah started to lob them at Parker, who deflected them with his staff, but even I could see that Micah had the upper hand in this battle and Parker was going to lose as soon as he ran out of steam.

Then it happened.

Micah used his flames to distract Parker as he dove in and gut checked Parker to the ground with twin swords at the ready to slice his throat open. When Micah didn't back off and I watched his hands tighten on the blades, I'd had enough. Breaking out of Jay's hold, I ran to the circle, and with a flair of power was able to pass right through, stumbling to my knees next to them. The absolute rage that was on Micah's face scared me, and the resigned look of acceptance from Parker broke my heart. He knew Micah would kill him without a second thought, and he felt like he deserved it for some godforsaken reason.

"Stop, please," I whispered, placing my hands over Micah's on the hilts of his swords. "I can't let you do this, Micah."

"Is it true?" Micah demanded through gritted teeth. "Did you accept his Oath?"

A tear trailed down my cheek as I looked deep into his sapphire eyes. "Yes, it's true."

His swords dissolved as the shutters closed over his emotions, cutting me off from him as if we were back to square one. My heart wrenched, and I didn't know how to stop him from walking away from me, because I needed to make sure Parker was alright. Loving more than one person was the best thing I'd ever experienced, but as I was learning in this moment, it could also be far more painful.

Before I could do or say anything, the door to the room burst open and a man gasping for air looked at us with wild eyes.

"Ubel has a chapel full of students trapped and is threatening to kill them all if Synergy doesn't come talk to him."

"Fuck!" Micah spat as he took off out the door, the rest of us hot on his heels.

Jay grabbed my hand, and we ran. Even though I had been put through the ringer today, the terror of knowing people's lives were held in the balance of me getting there in time to stop him fueled me. When I checked my power source, I noticed that it was replenished and still had small hints of silver floating through it. Seems that as we sealed the Oath, I'd pulled energy from him, and I couldn't be more grateful.

When we exited the underground facility, we were in a large hangar with Humvees and other military-grade equipment for missions. Micah was already behind the wheel of a tactical Jeep, and Jay tossed me up into the passenger seat as he hopped in the back. The other four piled into another Jeep since Micah already slammed on the gas, sending us rocketing out of the hangar into open pasture at the back of the property. Hanging on for dear life since there were no doors, seatbelts, or even fabric walls to keep us in, we drove over the rough ground.

When we reached campus, I saw more Elementi herding students away and blocking off the pathways to the quad where the chapel, now used as an auditorium, sat. It wasn't lost on me that Ubel had picked the chapel for this stunt since it was the beginning of what this university had turned into. The first stand Ryevick made against evil to teach and train others to fight against them. Now, knowing what and who I am, I wasn't at all surprised that I'd focused on that particular building to study when I first got here. It might have also been why Ubel was using it as his epic taunt towards me, knowing the history it represented.

Micah barely gave the guard time to pull the barrier out of our way as we sped through the walkways of the school, sliding to a stop in the middle of the quad. I stood in my seat, holding onto the roll cage of the Jeep and looking at the chapel in the glow of the setting sun. Tony and the others pulled in beside us moments later without all the screeching and smoking tires.

Up on the bell tower balcony, the doors were pulled open, and Ubel walked out. He didn't look the same, but I knew it was him. How I didn't see it before was shocking, but I'd only met the man once since the first time when I'd been delirious with demon venom running through my veins.

"Oh, I see you've finally connected the dots there, Synergy." Ubel grinned, leaning on the railing, looking down at us from Mr. Creed's face. "I have to admit, I was saddened that it was so easy to fool all of you. These so-called Knights should have known I wasn't the real Mr. Creed. They've spent years taking lessons from him. Especially that brooding Fire Knight of yours... such a pity."

Swearing and the sound of crumpling metal drew my attention down where Micah was wailing on the dash of the Jeep.

"That one would make an excellent vessel for Aeshma, the Greater Demon of Wrath, should he decide to awaken. Goodness, you might even be like me and just be blessed with one of the Greater Demons' powers as their conduit," Ubel chattered on.

"What do you want?" I called, unable to take his ramblings much longer.

Ubel's face and body started to shift and change until he looked like the man I met at the pond. "The Dark Lord warned me that you were stubborn, but I think it might be because you are just too stupid to understand what's going on. It's not about what *I* want—no, it's about what the Dark Lord *needs*. You see, your Spirit Knight was correct when he said that the Greater Demons were still sleeping and needed demonic energy to awaken and fulfill their work here on Earth. So how do we do that? Well, we take large groups of people and give them the serum, letting them welcome lesser demons into a new home. Oh! I almost forgot, I figured out a way to aerosolize it, giving us the ability to administer it to large amounts of people, much like this chapel full of students. For you, though, I think the old-fashioned way would be best—just think what it would be like if we injected you with the serum, being as powerful as you are? Would you be able to host one of our great Princes of Hell?"

All the dots started to connect. Each time the Dark Lord came to taunt me, he pushed me to see how much stronger I'd gotten since the last time we'd talked. When I proved that I could shield myself from him at least slightly, he'd left me alone and sent Ubel instead. The Dark Lord couldn't test me further as he was; he needed someone in person who could push me to gain strength to be of better use to them. If I gave myself up and let them inject the serum into me, it would bring down the rest of the walls of my own self-doubt and reservations, freeing me to be at my most powerful state.

"By the look of terror on your face, I see you fully understand what I'm talking about. How delightful! So, what's it going to be, Synergy? Am I going to take these two hundred innocent lives and turn them into the perfect vessels to feed our sleeping lords, or will you surrender to me?" Ubel questioned, giving me a smile that was more teeth than anything. "I'll give you some time to think it over. If you decide to surrender, all you have to do is call out my name and it will be a done deal. Don't take too long, though—I do get bored easily these days."

In a swirl of green smoke he was gone, leaving me with an impossible choice.

Crumpling back into my seat, I curled up into a little ball, trying to find any way out of this other than the obvious one.

CHAPTER 29

LAILAH

Arms wrapped around me, and I knew it was Brayden who pulled me from the Jeep and carried me. In our hurry to leave, none of us had grabbed our coats, and we certainly were not wearing warm clothes. The blast of heat told me he'd taken me inside somewhere, and lifting my head, I saw we were in the coffee shop. Brayden sat in one of the leather chairs with me on his lap; it was the same chairs that we sat in when we went on our first "date" that got crashed by the others. Now I was surrounded by them all, faced with an impossible choice.

"What are we going to do?" I whispered.

Micah leaned forward and grabbed my chin tightly, making me flinch a little as he forced me to look up at him. "I'll tell you what we aren't going to do, Lailah—give you up to them. That isn't an option, so don't waste your time thinking about it. There is only one of him and six of us, plus all of the Elementi we can muster. There is something we can do besides that."

Jay took a tablet from one of the Elementi security guards and started looking something over. "We need to think where the best place to put a device that would disperse the serum would be. If we can remove that part of the equation, it gives us a lot more ground to work with. I finally got word back from the labs and the employee file on the man who is now Ubel. He was indeed part of the team that helped create the serum, and I think he was a plant all along. His resume would be exactly what your father or the company as a whole would be looking for, making it easy for him to get the job."

"What is the air system like in the chapel?" Parker asked.

Micah glared at him over his shoulder. "This isn't some action flick where it would be that obvious. This man is clever and deceitful. Who knows if there really is a way to do what he said—demons lie, remember?"

"Okay ass-munch, at least one of us is coming up with ideas," Parker snapped back.

Nothing that happened in the circle made this any better. In fact, I think it made it worse. Micah was acting fine, but I knew I'd hurt him by not being honest and telling him that I'd taken Parker's Oath. I'd known in my gut when Parker asked me to keep it quiet that it wasn't the best choice, but I also understood where Parker was coming from. Shaking my head, I tossed those thoughts to the wayside—there were bigger things to deal with right now.

"Well, if we take that logic, do we think he even plans to do what he says to those students?" Hudson interjected.

"It's still winter break, so why are there so many people in the chapel?" Brayden asked, making us all pause.

Jay pulled a paper out of his back pocket and handed it over to us. "A guard found this posted around the school."

As I skimmed over the flier, it showed that there would be a free movie night with popcorn for those who were still on campus.

"That sick motherfucker planned this. Do we have any idea when these went up?" Micah questioned as he looked over the sheet.

"I can check the campus security feeds real quick, but that doesn't change the fact that it happened," Jay pointed out.

Sitting up straighter on Brayden's lap, I cleared my throat, drawing everyone's attention. "This is all good information, but it still isn't helping us figure out how to save them and kill Ubel."

"What if we just went in guns blazing, so to speak?" Parker suggested. "Look, I know most of you don't want to even look at me right now, but we have a job to do. We can sort out the personal shit later."

"It isn't the worst idea," Jay contemplated. "If we bust through the front doors, we can make sure that everyone has a chance to get out if he really has set the place up to be a dirty bomb. Then we can take the fight directly to him to keep him busy."

Hudson leaned forward, adjusting his glasses. "You're forgetting his ability to transport himself out. We need a ward up to perfect that kind of travel."

"There is one," Brayden said. "It's built into the wards surrounding the school that we recharged."

"We just saw him use it, though," Micah countered.

"Then it can only go a short distance. It would keep him trapped in the walls of the school property," Brayden answered.

Micah groaned and leaned back in his chair. "That still does nothing for us. He could just walk out of the barrier and use his transport skills then. All we have set up is for demons, not nut job humans with demonic powers. God, we are so fucked!"

"What we need is for someone to get a ward or shield around him so that we can keep him in one place long enough to stop or trap his powers. If we can disable them, then he is your average human again," Brayden reasoned.

I held up a hand, stopping the conversation. "Wait, I think we need to make sure we are all on the same page. Are we trapping him and keeping him alive or killing him?"

"The leadership would like to keep him alive to learn more

about the effects of the serum, but if we can't, then we are allowed to take him out," Jay answered, holding my gaze so I knew that he didn't like the order any more than I did.

"Was this another thing you guys were waiting to tell me about?" I demanded, irritation hot under my skin.

"No, Beautiful, we got the text on our way over here to the scene. Just didn't seem like a good time to tell you until now," Jay chided, causing me to realize I might have reacted a little too strongly.

Micah stood and started to pace. "I say damn what they want and do what needs to be done. None of us will lose any sleep over the fact this guy will be gone. Now, do we have any other bright ideas, or are we kicking down the door?"

"Oh, so you're saying that you like my idea?" Parker mused.

"Don't push it, Parker, or we will finish what I started in the ring, no matter what Lailah says," Micah growled, his dual swords appearing in his hands. "Let's get this over with. It's fucking freezing, and I don't like that Lailah doesn't have a coat."

With grim looks on all their faces, they stood and walked out, but Brayden didn't move, knowing I needed a moment before we did this.

"You okay, Angel?" Brayden asked, running a hand down my back.

"No, but does that really matter? This is what we have to do, and I have to agree with Micah—the world will be a safer place without that man in it." I sighed and gave him a peck on the lips before I stood, holding out a hand to him. "Come on, let's go save some lives and kick some demon ass."

Back out in the quad, that was now deserted for all but the six of us, we marched towards the chapel. Micah, in the lead, hit the chapel doors with two powerful blasts of fire, enough to knock the doors off their hinges, and Hudson followed up, putting the fire out before it could take hold. Jay used his wind to pull what debris he could from the entrance swiftly, leaving a clear path for people to leave by. When we entered the chapel, it was completely silent and far too dark until the overhead light blazed into existence.

"Oh, you dear, sweet, baby-minded Knights. Did you really think it would be that easy to get the drop on me? Now you have to find your precious students before it's too late. I got tired of waiting and started the clock ages ago," Ubel's disembodied voice called out. "Call my name any time, Synergy, and this will all end. Remember, whatever happens is on you."

Micah punched the stone wall at the same time Jay started to swear silently.

"What? What did we miss?" I pressed.

"The tunnels. They don't connect to anything anymore, but they are still under the chapel. This used to be where the Elementi would enter and exit the school for missions, but they are no longer needed with the new system," Jay muttered as he started knocking on the wood-paneled walls. "Come on guys, we need to find the entrance down to the tunnels... and fast."

We branched out, and I tried to remember what I read in those journals I found in the Elementi section of the school library. Then it hit me, and I raced to the back where the bell tower was. Ubel had picked that spot to meet us for more than one reason. Reaching the door to that section of the chapel, I found the handle was broken off and the lock jammed—this was it! Pulling my power to me, I tried to use my sai to stab around the lock to try and get it to break loose, but even though the wood was old, it was well crafted and maintained.

"Guys, I found it!" I called, hoping they could hear me.

I used my emotional connection to Brayden and Hudson to get them to come find me just in case they couldn't hear me all the way back here. When I wasn't getting anywhere fast, I dropped my sai and tried to create a ball of energy like I had when fighting Tabitha to see if that would work. When the blast hit the wood, it didn't damage the door. It did the opposite, bringing the door back to its original working order. I let out a whoop of excitement and turned the handle that was now unlocked and let me enter into the room with the spiral staircase leading up to the bells. On the floor was a trap door that I guessed led down to the tunnels.

I paused, unsure if I should keep going on my own or if waiting would be better. Then I heard the sound of feet running to me close by, and I knew they were on their way, so I headed for the trap door. Grasping the old steel ring, I pulled with all my might and got the door to budge but little else. I wasn't going to be able to do this on my own. Moments later, the guys burst in, panting as they paused to catch their breath.

"Look, I found it," I said with a smile, pointing to the trap door. "Guess being a nerd about the school was helpful this time."

Hudson walked over to me and kissed my forehead. "Sunshine, you are brilliant. Now, let's see if we can get this thing open."

It took three of them lifting and the other two pushing to break the rust on the hinges to get it open.

"Guess he didn't use this to get them down there," Brayden said, his chest heaving from the exertion.

"Let's just make sure we keep it open so we don't have to fight it getting everyone out," Hudson reasoned as we all peered down the hole.

There was an old wooden ladder, covered in cobwebs, built down one side of the tunnel. Micah walked over with a piece of wood in his hand that he lit on fire and dropped down into the tunnel. We watched and waited for it to hit the ground, letting us know how far this thing went. It dropped a good ten feet or so, and we could see the flickering of the flame, but it wasn't enough to give us light on our way down.

"Who gets the honor of going first?" Parker asked, looking between Jay and Micah.

Without a word, Jay climbed into the hole and started down the ladder, then went Brayden and Micah.

I started forward, but Hudson grabbed my arm. "Please, Sunshine, can you do us this one favor and stay up here?"

"Why?" I frowned, not liking this request at all. "We're a team. We need each other, Hudson."

He sighed and hung his head. "I know, I know, but would you be willing to compromise and let me go down first just in case? We still don't know if you have any offensive abilities with your powers. Everything so far has been defensive."

"Fine, I'll let you go first, but I'm going no matter what," I answered begrudgingly.

Hudson went next, and I waited a few moments to give them a little head start so I didn't crash into them on the way down. Then Parker took up the rear making sure nothing came at us from behind.

"The rest of us made it no problem!" Brayden called from below.

Hearing that set me at ease as my feet hit the first rung of the ladder, descending into the cool darkness of the tunnel. With no way of knowing how far I'd gone or still had to go, the journey took forever as I gingerly took each step down. I was worried if I moved too fast I might slip and fall or step on Hudson's hands, causing him to fall.

"You're doing great, Sunshine. Slow and steady," Hudson's voice echoed, soothing my fears. "I'm off the ladder, so you have nothing to worry about. Just keep coming."

When my feet hit the dirt floor, I sagged against the wall, relieved to have that part over with, only to be faced with the next task of where to go from here.

"Alright, we need to pair up. I sent a map of the tunnels that is believed to be the most accurate, but that's not guaranteed," Jay instructed as he also handed out flashlights and flares out of a backpack I didn't notice he had on. "Thank God we took the Jeeps so we had some kind of supplies to work with."

"Fuck, Jay, you always make the rest of us look like idiots when it comes to shit like this," Micah muttered as he took the flashlight and stuffed a few flares in his back pockets.

Jay just gave him a blank look and shrugged his shoulders. "Guess it comes with how I was raised."

Once we had everything we needed and split into two groups of three, we headed out. Jay, Parker, and Brayden went to the left and the rest of us went to the right with Hudson leading the way, the map in hand on his phone. Micah moved me to the middle of the group so he took up the rear, which was smart with my skills of getting lost in a cereal box.

The tunnels reminded me of photos that I'd seen of ancient catacombs chiseled into the earth, mason blocks holding up the walls and ceilings. Some sections had alcoves where old priests had been buried along with some of the early Elementi Knights. It was spooky and fascinating at the same time, but the reality of why we were down here kept things in perspective.

When we came to a domed room that was different from the others, far more lavish with intricate etchings in the stone walls, I couldn't help myself. I wandered over to see who it was that had been laid to rest here, gently dusting off the nameplate on the sarcophagus. *Here lies Aiden Ryevick.*

"Holy shit! You guys, this is the founder of Ryevick!" I gasped.

"We can come back to look, Lailah, but we need to stay on track," Micah whispered, harshly motioning me to follow.

Shaking my head, trying to get it back to the matters at hand, I trailed after them.

"Tick tock goes the clock, Synergy... how much time do they have left?" Ubel's voice echoed hauntingly down the tunnel behind me.

"It's this way!" I yelled as I took off, Hudson and Micah yelling at me to wait up.

I didn't wait, though—how could I when there were people trapped down here like sitting ducks for Ubel to play with? I wouldn't have any more blood on my hands over this; it was time I took a stand and say enough was enough. Ubel was not getting out of this alive; he posed too high of a risk, no matter what they did to try and keep his powers contained. He was sick and twisted, through and through.

His laughter echoed off the walls, leading me to him, and I ran faster, afraid he would slip through my fingers. Skidding to a halt, I came to the edge of a cliff where it looked like there had once been a stone bridge over an underground river. I looked around furiously, but I couldn't see any way to get around to the other side. I was at a dead end.

"You want so desperately to be treated like one of them, but look where that has gotten you," Ubel chided as he walked out of the tunnel behind me. "Foolish, simple minded, and so easily led astray. No wonder they wanted you to stay behind and out of the way, but did you listen? No. No, you did not—you never do."

Anger roared through me as he poked at all of my insecurities so casually. "Are there even people trapped down here?"

"Oh yes, but they are nowhere near here," Ubel said as he began to circle around me. "I just needed to get you away from the others so we could have a heart to heart."

"What could I possibly have to talk to you about?" I snapped.

"Just the lives of the five men you love and two hundred innocents that will all perish once the bombs go off and collapse these shoddy old tunnels. They really should have kept them up or filled them in."

My hands clenched into fists, nails biting into my palms. "You're lying."

Ubel rolled his eyes at me and produced a remote detonator, wagging it in front of me. "See, I'm not the type who bluffs. I enjoy killing far too much for that. Only, I get a win-win out of this situation. Either you give yourself up to me and the Dark Lord, or I blow everyone up and let the blast trigger large containers of the weaponized serum that will spread around the whole school and even the town. Think of all the hundreds and thousands of people I would be able to infect."

The glee that I saw flashing in his eyes led me to believe every word he said was true. In his mind, he did win either wayn. Now it was left up to me to decide how this would all end.

CHAPTER 30

BRAYDEN

"I don't like that we split up from the others," Parker grumbled as we reached another fork in the path. "What happens when they find everyone? If we are underground, how is that going to work?"

Jay stopped in the middle of the tunnel and turned on Parker, thrusting something into his hands. "They have one of these and will be able to radio us if they find anything, even if we are underground. Now, looking at the map, it would be more likely Ubel is keeping them all in this large open area here. So let's mark the wall and head to the right."

"Great. Now even you're being a dick about things. What did I do wrong this time?" Parker muttered under his breath.

Typically, Parker never pissed me off, but how he was dealing with things, especially telling Lailah to keep things secret, had gone too far. Now I wish I was like Micah and didn't give a shit if I punched the big baby in his face.

"I think if you were more focused on the mission and not worried about yourself, it might help," I suggested as I shoved passed him.

Parker tossed his hands in the air. "How is being worried about Lailah not being focused?"

"Because we ALL worry about Lailah!" I yelled, turning to face him again. "Don't you get it? All of us love that woman, and if anything happened to her, it would kill each and every one of us. *But*—I know that if we let anything happen to these innocent people, it will break something in her that we may not be able to fix. So, getting these people to safety is my top priority right now because it's hers—you get it now?"

Parker looked at me, stunned. I don't think any of them had really seen me lose my temper before, but everyone had a breaking point. I knew that both Micah and Hudson would do whatever it took to keep Lailah safe, and through our bond I also knew she was fine, even if I couldn't be with her.

Seeing that Parker didn't have anything else to add, I started after Jay as he led us deeper into the catacombs. Now moving in silence, I was able to pick up on the sound of people whispering and others crying softly. When we emerged into the large open area that looked like it at one point had been a gathering room of sorts, we found the students. All their hands and feet were bound, and many of them were still knocked out, laying on the ground, while a few others had managed to huddle together.

I jogged over to one, pulling the gag from his mouth before I started on his hands. "Are you alright?"

"Fuck if I know, I can't even remember what happened or how I got down here. Where are we?" he asked, rubbing his wrists once they were free.

"Under the chapel in the catacombs. We've come to get you guys out, but sit tight until we've checked on the others. You could get lost really easily out there," I reassured as I moved on to the person next to him.

Quickly, the three of us worked, and a few of the other students helped as well once free. The ones that were still asleep needed Parker's particular skill to wake them up from the demon magic used on them. Now that everyone was awake, a group off in one corner seemed to start panicking about something.

"There's a BOMB!" a girl screamed, setting off the whole room.

"Oh my god, there's another over here! We're all gonna die down here, aren't we?!" another voice called.

I looked at Jay, unsure of what to do but hoping he had some experience with what was going on. Nodding to me, he let out a shrill whistle that he amplified with his power so it boomed through the room, causing everyone to stop and look at him.

"If you want to make it out of here alive, then you need to calm down," Jay instructed. "Give us a moment to see what's going on before we set something off by accident. The best thing we can do is remain calm."

This seemed to settle some people, but others were in hysterics and tried to fight to get out of the room. Jay signaled to Parker, who nodded his head and sent out a wave of power, putting everyone back to sleep. It was the safest option we had with only three of us trying to deal with everything.

"*Guys, do you read me?*" Hudson's voice sounded over the radio.

Parker pulled the device out of his back pocket and hit the button to talk. "Yeah, we hear you."

"*We lost Lailah...*"

"What the fuck did he say?!" I snarled, yanking the radio out of Parker's hand. "You better be lying to me, Hudson."

"*Trust me, I wish I was too. She said something about hearing Ubel and took off in the opposite direction from us and vanished. We're still looking for her, but I don't think we can manage without you guys.*"

"How much you wanna bet that bastard planned this?

There's no way we can help them if we have bombs set to go off in this room," Parker pointed out as he turned to slam his fists into the wall. "Damn it, damn it, damn it all to hell."

"Did you just say there were bombs?" Micah's voice asked over the radio. *"That evil prick never planned on us getting out of this place alive, did he?! Damn it! I bet he lured Lailah away from us as leverage—FUCK!"*

I looked around the room, torn on what to do next. We needed to get these people out of here before something happened... but what about Lailah?

"We need a group decision on how to handle this, guys. On one hand, we have two hundred students trapped underground surrounded by bombs. On the other, Lailah is missing and probably in the clutches of a psycho demonic murderer." I said, watching Jay and Parker for any sign of what they thought we should do as we waited for Hudson and Micah to weigh in.

Parker's shoulders sagged as I saw him come to a choice. "We need to do what we can to protect them. It's what she would want us to do if she was here. Have Micah and Hudson keep looking for her, but we can't abandon them. I couldn't look her in the face if we chose her over all of them."

"He's right. If you two keep working on your end, we will handle this," Jay agreed, talking into the radio. "If we get things squared away here, it will give us all the time we need to keep looking for her with you guys, but live bombs in play jeopardizes us all."

I could hear muttering through the radio as they talked before Hudson gave us their answer. *"We are both in agreement with you, Jay. I have a connection with her, so that will help keep us going in the right direction, and you guys are on the opposite end of the catacombs as it is. Deal with the bombs and the students, and we will keep you informed of what's happening on our end as we can."*

"Check back in fifteen minutes if you don't hear from us

before that," Jay relayed as he stuffed the radio in his back pocket. "Okay, let's go take a look at what we're dealing with."

Spreading out, we walked along the edge of the room and found a total of five bombs, each of them having an additional canister on them with what we speculated was the demon serum.

"Alright, so I can defuse these bombs, but I don't have all the tools I need to do it quickly," Jay started, causing us both to groan. "That means I need you two to help me since I'm working with a multi-tool instead of the specialized bomb kit we have for these circumstances. The other part of this I should be honest about is that I've never deactivated a bomb like this on my own. I've assisted one of our techs and seen it done, just not on my own."

"We just aren't going to catch a break on this, are we?" I asked, looking over the bomb. "There's no other option. We have to do something, and having some idea how to do this is better than none. What do you need from us?"

Jay took a deep breath and rubbed his face with his hands. This might be the first time I'd ever seen him nervous about anything.

"Let's see if we can move it away from the wall so I can get a better look at it," Jay said, grabbing part of the bomb.

Parker's head snapped in Jay's direction. "I'm sorry, what? You want us to move this device that could go off at any time? Nope, sorry, I want to live."

"Then I suggest you help and give us the best chance of keeping your sorry ass alive," I growled, taking the other side, but the way it was shaped, it kept tilting forward, totally off balance.

Parker stepped up and grabbed the front, steadying it as we shuffled away from the wall and set it back down.

"Okay, now I need all the light I can without any shadow.

One wrong cut wire and I'll blow us all the fuck up," Jay explained as he handed me his flashlight.

Pulling out his tool, he slowly worked at getting off the top of the bomb, showing all the wires. It was a massive, chaotic ball of wire that you couldn't tell what was going where. The rat bastard had taken every opportunity to make this as hard as possible. Jay picked through the wires and was able to sort out what was real and what was just jumbled up in there. Finally, he cut a wire and crossed it with another before cutting two more. The small timer showed up, giving us five minutes before it would go off. Not having the right tool, he needed to use the blade to get the small screws out of the plate at the bottom, eating into our time before he revealed a small tube of liquid.

"You have got to be kidding me!" Jay swore, rubbing his forehead as he looked down at the bomb. "It doesn't make sense why he would have three backup triggers!"

"Talk to us Jay, what's going on?" I asked, trying to understand what I was looking at.

Jay glanced up at me, worry filling his eyes. "Either this was put here to cause whoever tried to disarm the bomb to panic and let the timer run out, or we have a major problem. This is a liquid trigger. If I mess with it too much, the two fluids will mix and react, causing it to blow up."

"Wait, but wouldn't it have done that when we moved it?" Parker questioned, squatting to look down at it closer. "I say it's a fake out, because at this point there's no other option. You have to remove that to get to the wire under it that controls the power to the battery."

"How the fuck do you know that?" Jay demanded, brows furrowed.

"Um..." Parker shrugged his shoulders "You guys keep forgetting I'm a technology guy. I get circuitry, and the way this is set up doesn't support a liquid trigger."

"Parker, if I do this, know that I'm trusting you with all our lives here. Do you still want me to break this?" Jay asked, his tone dead serious.

Leaning even closer and looking at a few things, Parker looked back at both of us and nodded his head. "Yes, I'm absolutely positive."

CHAPTER 31

LAILAH

Here I was, standing on the edge of a cliff, a plunge into the river below my only choice if I didn't want to deal with the evil, demonic man in front of me. Would I choose to fight knowing that I would put everyone's lives in danger, or would I make the hard choice and surrender? No matter what choice I made, I lost, but I couldn't see any other option.

Okay, there was a third option, but martyrdom was not at the top of the list either.

"I can see how much this choice weighs on you. How about I put a time limit on things?" Ubel offered. "Personally, I find that the threat of death really clears the mind and shows you what your heart truly wants. There is no second-guessing when you just let pure instinct take over. So you have five minutes to make your choice before I push this detonator and trigger the bombs."

Ubel made a big show of pulling out a phone and setting the timer, placing it on the ground so that I could clearly see the time ticking away. Dropping to my knees on the ground, I covered my face with my hands, wracking my brain to find some way that I could get out of this situation that I just wasn't seeing.

What would happen if I fought him? All I needed to do was get the trigger away from him, and that would give everyone more time. No, that was stupid. He could just poof away from me and set the bombs off then.

Okay, well, what would giving in do? Oh, sure the Dark Lord said he would save my men, but that didn't mean he changed his plans for everyone else getting wiped off the face of the planet or turned into demon bodysuits. *Think, Lailah, think!*

Then the flicker of an idea crossed my brain. It was risky and foolish and probably would get me hurt or killed. What other option did I really have, though?

"Okay, I have an answer for you," I said, looking up from where I knelt.

Ubel squatted down in front of me with a grin on his face. "Speak quickly. You only have a minute left."

"I surrender to the Dark Lord," I whispered, unable to utter the words any louder. My heart twisted and despair rolled over me, knowing that I never had another choice to make than this.

Before I could even react, Ubel slipped a syringe out of his pocket and injected me with the serum. "Welcome to the family, Synergy. I can't wait to see what happens next!"

Pain burst through my body, much like it had when I was attacked by the demons on our scouting mission months ago. This time, though, I felt it scorching over every nerve, altering my cells, and even slowing my pulse as I was being morphed into a new being. Gasping, I clawed at the dirt floor as my body spasmed, fighting against the toxin, ripping a scream from my lungs. All the while, Ubel watched with excitement, even clapping his hands at one point. Once the serum had done its damage, I lay sprawled out on the ground, coated in sweat and lungs heaving.

What had I done?

"Rest a moment. That first dose really does a number on ya,"

Ubel crooned, patting the top of my head. "Close your eyes. I'm sure the Dark Lord will want to talk with you."

As if he'd used some sort of power on me, I drifted off to sleep, and sure enough, I found myself in that void where the Dark Lord always found me.

"Oh, my Little Synergy, I'm so glad to see that you've come to your senses and realized this is for the best. Although I admire how you made me work much harder than I anticipated to get you to see reason. Ubel tried to tell me you were a lost cause and I should just kill you and the others while I could. Now, here you are," the Dark Lord cheered as he gathered me up in his arms, my body still unable to move. The smell of sulfur and smoke curled around me, almost choking me with the acrid scent. "We have a very special person for you to meet. Unfortunately, she is still asleep, but you are going to fix that, much like Ubel is with Dantalion."

It felt as though I was being pulled through a thick substance, every sense registering in slow motion. I couldn't see well, but this time I could see the outline of objects like I was still underground in the dark. This was not the catacombs I'd left behind, though. This was somewhere totally different that set my hairs on end. A soft, light-green light glowed in the distance, growing brighter as we approached, and finally I could see a woman laying on a stone slab much like I'd seen for the preparation of burial. Only this woman looked very much alive, just deep in slumber.

"This is the mother of all, Lady Lilith. She was punished by the Seven Princes of Hell because she wanted to free all her children and let them own the Earth as was their right," the Dark Lord intoned as he laid me down next to her on the stone slab. "You have been chosen to carry her essence so that you will become her conduit to gain her powers back. Once the All Mother is back with us, then our plan can proceed, even without the support of the Princes and the other Greater Demons."

I looked up at the Dark Lord, and even with empty voids where his eyes should have been, I could tell he was looking tenderly upon Lilith. Was this whole thing just a way to gain favor with the one woman he couldn't have? Destroy the Earth so that Lilith and her children could be free from Hell or wherever this was?

The Dark Lord paused and listened. I could hear sounds in the distance, as if someone was heading our direction. Quickly he turned back to me, grabbing Lilith's arm and holding it over my face. Taking a claw, he cut her wrist, letting her blood splatter all over my face and body as he chanted. The blood started to burn and smoke against my skin, causing me to scream until I felt like my voice was going to be raspy forever.

The Dark Lord didn't stop. He ignored me and proceeded with whatever ritual he was doing, blending in some of his own blood for good measure, which felt like more acid being dripped onto my skin. Rage contorted his face as he spoke louder, forcing more power into his actions. Then he started to make small cuts into my flesh, drawing jagged symbols just like I'd seen on the poor woman's body on stage. Just when I didn't think this could hurt any more than it already did, it ratcheted up to another level of pure agony. All I could do was pray that I would pass out or just be killed so it would stop.

"Why won't this work," the Dark Lord bellowed, his anger so strong that his words shook the ground around us. "I don't have enough time for this not to work. You accepted this fate, been given the serum, you should be *mine.*"

"No, never yours. I belong to them," I rasped out, tears streaming from my face as the pain lessened.

The Dark Lord leaned over me, his sharp black teeth gnashing in front of me, his saliva dripping from his chin on to my face. "This cannot be! You are not Bonded to them all, you can still be taken. More serum, that's what you need. I will send you back to Ubel and he will give you another dose—yes, that's it. You are just too strong to be defeated by one dose. That has to be it."

Seconds later, I felt as if the Dark Lord had picked me up like a football and chucked me back into reality, causing my eyes to burst open and my lungs to gasp for breath like I'd been drowning.

"It didn't work. Why? Why wouldn't it work? I made the perfect serum, what have you done?" Ubel asked before he froze. "No, Dark One, don't take me under..."

Ubel's eyes became vacant, and he crumbled to the ground like he was absent from his body.

Now. It needed to happen now, or none of us were going to live through this.

Rolling over, I dragged myself over to him, knowing this was going to be my only chance to end this particular nightmare for good. Shoving Ubel over onto his back, I straddled his hips, sobbing at the pain of forcing my battered body to move. Reaching inward, I called my powers forward, pulling strength from Hudson and Brayden's presence, forever a part of me, and the tentative connections I had with Jay and Parker waiting to be completed.

Gathering all the love they'd each given me, the comforting touches and reassurance that I was always stronger than I believed, I plunged that right into Ubel's heart, guiding it with the razor-sharp tip of my sai. Ubel bucked under me, trying to fight me off, the demonic connection in him screeching at me, attacking every insecurity that I had, ripping my soul apart as he tried to cling to this body in the hope it would still free him.

"You are not welcome here, Dantalion, nor is any other who plans to destroy my home or the people I love. Make sure to tell everyone in the pit of Hell you call home that the Elementi Knights will not fail in their mission and we will take on anyone who gets in our way," I vowed, sending another surge of power crashing into him. I felt all six of our powers flowing through me, casting Dantalion back to where he came from, severing him from his conduit. Unable to handle the power flowing through me, I released my sai and fell to the side, crying and shaking as I met Marvin's gaze for the first time.

"You might have killed me, but I'm not the only one..." he gasped as I watched the light go out in his eyes.

Curling up, I took his still warm hand and let my grief take over, knowing I had done the right thing but also knowing that I was responsible for his death.

This was the thing that people who've been in war say you never understand until you've experienced it. Marvin Brown, evil as he may have been, was still a casualty of war. A man who had done unspeakable things, some I'm sure we still had yet to discover. I'd been charged with keeping this world and the people in it safe from men and demons like him, but his death would always be on my hands. The angels, the Elementi, and even my guys would forgive me and tell me I did nothing wrong —but I would carry it with me forever. That was the cost, and I was willing to pay it, but for the sake of my soul, I prayed I didn't need to do it often.

"We found her and she's alive," Micah shouted, pulling me out of my haze to look up at him. "God, what have they done to you, sweetheart?"

Hudson came rushing out of the tunnel with the radio up to his face, talking quickly to someone on the other end. "Micah found her. We're by the underground river. Looks like the bridge collapsed. We are gonna need a medical team, though—she's covered in blood."

"*What do you mean she's covered in blood?!*" Brayden demanded. "*I'm going to need a little more information than that after what we've been through. God, it wasn't even happening to me and I thought I was gonna die."*

Micah gently pulled Marvin's hand out of my grasp and lifted me up, bridal style, close to his chest. "Let's get you out of here," he murmured, pressing his lips to the top of my head.

I clutched onto the fabric of his t-shirt as he turned to head back into the tunnels. "Wait! There's bombs! He had the deto-nator—we might need that."

"Shh, it's fine," Micah soothed as he kept walking at a fairly quick pace.

"The other three disabled the bombs and have almost gotten everyone out. We were able to make a larger exit from a tunnel closer to the surface with the help of the teams on the outside," Hudson informed me, freeing me from the last thing I needed to worry about before I passed out again.

I was safe... for now. But the battle was far from over.

To be continued in *Taming Fire*

About the Author

Elizabeth is originally from Illinois but is now living in sunny Phoenix, Arizona. Though she is newer to publishing, Elizabeth has been writing for nine years. She started in YA Fiction but recently found herself loving the Reverse Harem genre. Like her favorite books, Elizabeth loves to write about strong women of all varieties. Not all strength is flashy or apparent at first glance some lie just under the surface.

Don't Miss Out!

Be the first to know what is coming next by following Elizabeth's social media! You never know when or what will be coming next!

Website: ElizabethKnightBooks.com

Facebook: Elizabeth Knight's Unicorn Queens

Instagram: elizabethknightauthor

Newsletter: sign up here

Also by Elizabeth Knight

Omegaverse

<u>Knot All Is</u>

Knot All Is Lost Duet - Complete

Knot All Is Ruined Duet - Complete

<u>Sunshine & Rainbows Omegaverse</u>

Bailey-Rose duet:

Clouds & Daydreams + Petals & Promises

Lyra/Eli duet:

Knot Now Knot Ever + Yes Now Yes Forever

Mafia Royalty Shared World

<u>Caprioni Queen</u>

Glitter & Guns

Blood & Heartache

Revenge & Truth

Love & Power

<u>Gun Runner Princess</u>

One For The Money

Two For The Show

Complete Series

<u>Hidden Empire Series</u>

Two Tricks

Three Tricks

Four Tricks

More Tricks

Our Tricks

<u>Hidden Empire Novel</u>

Harper's Renegades

[Read after Four Tricks for best series context]

Omega Assassin

Dual Nature

Hidden Nature

Perfect Nature

-

<u>Hope Series</u>

Hidden Hope

Claiming Hope

Defending Hope

Obtaining Hope

-

Standalones

Nicolette - MC Feline Shifter Story

Lying Lainey - Dark Omegaverse

Books Not in Kindle Unlimited

<u>Elementi Series</u>

Discovering Synergy

Refining Earth

Liberating Water

Taming Fire

Rescuing Air

<u>Mercenary Queen Series</u>

Birthright

Dragon Queen

Forgotten Throne

The Final Battle

www.ingramcontent.com/pod-product-compliance
Lightning Source LLC
Chambersburg PA
CBHW060310310726
48976CB00007B/2279